Hailey Staker is a military photojournalist who joined the Air Force to tell its stories and travel the world. With the Air Force, she spent two years on Okinawa, Japan, where she met her husband. Born and raised in Central Texas, Hailey now lives in South Dakota with her husband, daughter, and their two dogs.

For Bridger and Adilynd, may your dreams always come true.

Hailey Staker

THE FURY'S LIGHT

AUSTIN MACAULEY PUBLISHERS™

LONDON • CAMBRIDGE • NEW YORK • SHARJAH

Ordering Information:
Quantity sales: special discounts are available on quantity purchases by corporations, associations, and others. For details, contact the publisher at the address below.

Publisher's Cataloging-in-Publication data
Staker, Hailey
The Fury's Light

ISBN 9781645754282 (Paperback)
ISBN 9781645754299 (Hardback)
ISBN 9781645366850 (ePub e-book)

Library of Congress Control Number: 2019908019

The main category of the book — Fiction / Fantasy / Urban

www.austinmacauley.com/us

First Published (2019)
Austin Macauley Publishers LLC
40 Wall Street, 28th Floor
New York, NY 10005
USA

mail-usa@austinmacauley.com
+1 (646) 5125767

I would like to thank my critique partners Rachel Buitrago, Chris Diaz, and Teresa Stine for telling me straight, as well as keeping me humble. To my editor, Amanda Hazel, for falling in love with these characters just as much as I did. My mother and father for their love, encouragement, and support that one day I would be published. To my husband, Bridger, who has supported me since the day we met on that small island in the East China Sea.

And in that moment, she saw the light, the light of which she was to become and that terrified her, for she felt no pain, saw nothing, heard only silence.

– The Fury's Light

Chapter 1

Blood gushed from her femoral artery, her skin turning white as a ghost.

"I'm...cold," she stuttered, her entire being shuddering.

The man, who never named himself, ripped her sweater until he had a strip long enough to tie right above the wound as a tourniquet.

"You never should have hit me," his voice was strained. "This wasn't supposed to happen."

He kept repeating the last sentence over and over. She grabbed his hands.

"Stop," she whispered. "Just let me die, please."

"No, you're coming with me, I just have to...wake up," his voice turned feminine and his hands were no longer around her leg but on her shoulders. "Lana, wake up."

Gray eyes with dilated pupils stared up at brown doe eyes. "I guess we're both having bad dreams still."

Lana rubbed her eyes, sitting up against the headboard, hair sticking to her neck and forehead, "Rae, how did you and your mom find me?"

"My visions...but that's over now, we have bigger things to worry about," Rae said. "We don't have much longer till they find you here."

Rae meant the hunters who worked for the one simply named 'Leader of the Darkness.' No matter where she went, she'd meet at least one who suspected her of being the one they were searching for, the Light Fury. On one hand, yes, she was supposedly this Light thing. On the other hand, the other people like her, the Furies, couldn't or didn't want to find the Fire Fury, so she could complete her training.

A Fury, she'd explained to Rae, was an elemental being who controlled a single base element, either Earth, Air, Fire, or Water. They were each tasked with teaching her how to conjure each of their elements, as the Light Fury was supposed to be able to conjure them all.

"It's a stupid prophecy thing apparently," Lana dismissed.

At least if the Darkness found her here, in Clover Bay where she first found out about her powers, she'd have the upper hand, know the lay of the land.

"What did you see?" Lana asked, though the memory from a week ago in Colorado still burned her eyes.

"You were being strangled by someone in black. I couldn't see their face," Rae said slowly, tucking a piece of light brown hair behind her ear. "But I could see yours, and you weren't fighting back."

Rae was a Seer, a being who sees snippets of the future but is rarely able to act upon them. Visions didn't come easily to her. Before she met Lana, she knew what she was, but not how to control and recall her visions. With a witch for a mother, one would think she had been trained or, at the very least, informed.

"It was night…and you were in a forest," Rae continued.

"There's the lake," Lana shrugged. "Or up the mountain."

"But why would you be out there so late?" Rae asked. They hadn't spent time with each other in more than five years, but Rae knew her better than anyone. Lana had always chosen to stay inside more often than not and Rae had to pry her from the window in the living room to get her out of the house. "I mean there'd have to be something going on that would cause you to go out of your way."

"When is the bonfire?" Lana asked. Rae climbed over the heaps of pillows covering Lana's duvet to her desk, plucking the college orientation folder from its perfectly poised position.

"Right after rush," Rae said, sifting through the jumble of papers in the folder for incoming freshmen. She pulled out a purple-and-gold-themed schedule outlining extracurricular activities, festivals, booths, fairs and orientation days for inbound students attending Clover Bay University.

"Today is the 17th," Lana mumbled.

"The day before orientation," Rae finished. Every year, Jacobs Lake held a bonfire during Rush, and it just so happened to be six days from now.

"I need to make a call," Lana stated, grabbing her phone from the nightstand.

"I'll see you later for coffee," Rae left the room, leaving the schedule on the bed.

"Yeah," Lana mumbled, scrolling through the contacts to those beginning with D and selected the first name under the category.

"This is Dimitri," the voice on the phone stated after three rings.

"I'm sorry, I have the wrong number," Lana said calmly, ending the call.

~

Buttery garlic, its salty, bold aroma filled the air. A tall blond man with emeralds for eyes hunched over the island in the center of the kitchen.

"Was that her?" his wife asked, her words alerting the black-haired boy behind him at the stove.

The dial tone resounded over the sizzling of garlic cloves in hot butter, a tired voice answering after just one ring.

"What do you want?" he asked.

"Clover Bay will soon be the devil's playground," Dimitri stated. "Prepare yourselves. Ensure you and Christine are primed."

"Why are you calling me?"

"Because you're the missing link, Aiden," Dimitri said. The call disconnected as garlic burned. Dimitri spun around, grabbing and throwing the skillet in the sink beside the stove. "We need to alert the Elders."

The black-haired boy spoke, "And tell them what? That Aiden is throwing his tantrums again? The Bay can't handle what's coming."

"And you think I don't know that, Wiley?" Dimitri turned toward his friend. "We all know what he is going to do when he finds out, and we will need the Elders there to ensure Lana is fully trained. Call them, now. And never step to me again."

Chapter 2

Clover Bay University sat on the northern edge of town surrounded by coffee shops, some bakeries, a Poncheros Mexican restaurant, and a small pub. Founded in 1838, just two years before the vampire infestation, the university was built entirely of stone, the buildings including vast archways, stained glass windows, and Victorian-era paintings across its ceilings.

Lana met Rae at The Hideout, the smallest coffee joint closest to the outskirts of town and owned by a good friend of Lana's, though she hadn't seen him the past few weeks since she came back to town.

"Did you have any more visions last night?" Lana whispered over Rae's shoulder as she came around to her chair. They sat at a petite metal circular table with white and purple orchids as its centerpiece.

"Keep it down! People can hear you when you talk like that," Rae said, cupping her hand over her mouth so her words were aimed directly at her friend.

"Covering your mouth only makes you look more suspicious," Lana smiled, mocking Rae. "So, are there any booths you want to check out after orientation?"

"I was thinking of skipping the festival and just heading home," Rae said. "I think we need to keep our heads low and just hang out until we absolutely have to be out and about."

"Well we have to go to the festival if we want to rush. And besides, it's not like they're going to attack in broad daylight," Lana said, taking a sip of her coffee. "They know better."

"How do you know *they* know better?" Rae asked.

"It's someone from the Darkness coming to make sure I'm actually where I am and all he's going to do is take me back to his master."

"You say that like it's a good thing…"

The porcelain cup scraped against metal. "I didn't say I'd actually let them win."

Rae kept quiet, flipping through her folder again for the list of booths present after orientation.

"So, Beta Psi and Alpha Theta will be at the festival, as well as the debate team, chess club…" Rae said.

"Lame. We can check out the sororities and maybe debate. Are there any other activities you want to check out after orientation?" Lana asked, Rae turning pages in the school catalog. "Rae?"

"What? Oh…" Rae stumbled, her vision focused on the book. "There's this…journal on campus. The staff writes about what's going on and puts out a publication of everyone's writing each semester."

Writing wasn't Lana's strong suit; she blamed it on her lack of formal education when she was a child. Most village children were homeschooled if their parents were around, though Lana's father was a lumberjack and her mother a seamstress. Instead, she and Donovan worked in the fields with other children whose parents worked full-time.

"That sounds right up your alley," she said, taking another sip of her latte.

"What are you going to take?" Rae asked.

"Art."

"Don't take this the wrong way or anything but you have to get out of your comfort zone," Rae laughed. "Everywhere you go, art."

"Sometimes you need a little consistency in your life," Lana shrugged.

Rae's eyes rolled so quickly Lana thought she was about to have a vision.

"I'm serious. You can't learn something new if you never try!" Rae preached.

"You sound like me," Lana smiled.

"Well, maybe you should take your own advice sometime," Rae said, stuffing the catalog back in its folder.

"Is everything alright?" Lana asked, setting her cup down with a clink.

"Yeah, why wouldn't it be?" Rae said, her voice shaky. "Let's get to the theater so we can get a seat closest to the entrance."

Lana followed her friend, for all she knew, this could be how they came these days. Rae's visions used to cause severe pain in her neck and would move down her spine, incapacitating her. Her eyes would roll back until nothing but white appeared and she'd faint, only to wake ten seconds later, after a brief glimpse flashed of an event soon to take place.

It seemed lately they came in the form of nightmares, shaking her to the core, shaking her so much she would need to wake Lana in order to calm down. Rae didn't ask for her powers, and Lana knew that, but something about Rae being able to see into the future, even for a brief period, made her valuable. It only took five years of coaxing Rae to use her powers for her to finally see farther than a few minutes or hours prior.

This ability allowed Lana the awareness of an attack from the Darkness, and that knowledge, although terrifying, was enough to convince her to see past Rae's flaws and keep the young Seer around.

Just outside the coffee shop, Rae stopped, her left hand clenching onto her folder. Lana walked around her, shielding her friend's dead stare from passers-by. Rae's dark brown eyes stared past Lana, her mouth open slightly as if a ghost had stolen her voice. The wind picked at pieces of her light brown hair, thin strands tickling her cheeks.

"Get out of the way, people are trying to walk here," a man in a business suit heading toward the real estate office bumped Lana's shoulder.

Rae exhaled, dry eyes trailing behind the walker. "Who was that and why were they being so rude?"

"What did you see?" Lana asked, her left arm hooking into Rae's right.

"I don't know, it was hard to make out," Rae said. "There was light, but it was blurry. And what looked like people's shadows. It's probably nothing. It didn't give me bad vibes like the other night."

Drop it, Lana thought as they headed toward the university.

Chapter 3

Dozens of young adults entered the 200-max-capacity auditorium, filling up the seats closest to the entrance.

"Don't be shy, I'm going to need some of you to come closer," a man with dark eyes and light blond hair said. He wore khakis and a light blue button-up with the top buttons undone. Waving his hands, the man continued to urge those attending his lecture to come forward.

Rae and Lana stayed in the back row, the latter refusing to move closer. "C'mon, he can't be that bad," the Seer said, grabbing hold of Lana's arm.

The girls made their way closer to the front, taking aisle seats about seven rows from where the lecturer stood. Instead of a tall stage, the room faded until a gazebo beside a river came into view.

A man with blond hair rested his chin on his hands, his elbows digging into his thighs. He looked up with hazel eyes, smiling warily when he saw her. With light brown hair cut into a short bob, the front touching her collarbone, she kissed his cheek lightly. He pulled a small wooden picture frame from his back pocket, holding it up in front of her face. A woman with her facial features and long dark brown curls standing next to a man with dark brown hair and high cheekbones filled the frame. Her interrogator grabbed hold of her arm tightly, his eyes asking who she really was, why the photo was so aged.

"Welcome to Clover Bay University," he said, his smooth voice breaking her free from her reverie. "My name is Professor Kyle Thomas, and I'll be giving you all a brief run-down of what we do here, what *here* is, and provide a tour of the campus afterward."

"Clover Bay never saw it coming," the professor began. "The town had only existed for five years when its reputation was tarnished.

"In 1840, the mayor found citizens of his town were disappearing and the local authorities blamed it on what they believed were animal attacks," Professor Thomas said. "What they didn't know at the time was their population was bleeding out, feeding a supernatural being until finally the beasts were caught and burned!"

Fire shot out from a cannon behind the man, many of the school's prospective students jumped out of their seats. Professor Thomas laughed.

"Now that I have your attention," he said. "You didn't think I was serious, did you? Vampires don't exist. But what does exist is a wonderful town with a rich history of taking care of its people when it matters most and even when it doesn't. I came to the Bay five years ago, and despite its small-town nature, you never know what you are going to come across."

He continued as he paced in front of the stage. Old Victorian mansions close to campus had been renovated and turned into sorority and fraternity homes, and the lake north of town was notorious for its perfectly flat coast of which hosted a driftwood bonfire every year.

"For those who believe Greek life is for them, just outside the entrance there are four booths for the Greek houses on campus," Professor Thomas stated. "If you have not received a tour of the campus, please meet me at the back of the auditorium. Congratulations on your acceptance to Clover Bay University, and don't let the vampires bite."

Lana was one of the first to stand and scoot her way past Rae. Professor Thomas's eyes followed the young Fury and Seer until their frames disappeared into the mass of students exiting the building. Rae grabbed hold of Lana's arm and pulled her toward the sorority tables to the right of the auditorium doors.

The girls standing at the table looked them up and down, "Welcome to Clover Bay U, my name is Vanessa and this is Alexa. We're sophomores here and oversee recruiting for Beta Psi. Are you ladies interested in joining a sorority?"

Lana's mind remained preoccupied with thoughts of Professor Thomas, knowing he stood just a few steps behind her with other students preparing to take their campus tour.

"Yes, we are," Rae said, tugging on Lana's arm. "I'm Rae and this is Lana."

"Well, it's certainly nice to meet you both! Beta Psi has around fifty girls currently, but we are always looking to add incoming freshmen. Our motto, which was originally penned by our founding sister Abigale Jenkins, is the more the merrier," Vanessa smiled. "Please take a brochure and keep us in mind while you rush next week!"

Rae took two pamphlets and led Lana away from the booth. They walked, elbows linked, through the festival until Rae spotted the newspaper booth across the common area.

"Go, I can handle myself," Lana said, squeezing Rae's arm.

"Is everything okay?" Rae asked. "You've been acting weird since we got here."

"You didn't even recognize him," Lana sighed. "That was Kyle. When he found out about me, he freaked!"

"Oh, I forgot about that," Rae's eyes met her feet. "At least he hasn't confronted you yet."

Lana shook her head and shrugged, her friend taking a few steps back. "I'll catch up with you in a bit."

She turned and walked past a few more booths until stopping at the art booth. It sat empty except for a few painted canvases of various posed models. A young man with his hair swept to the right approached from her left before hopping over the empty table next to them.

"Like what you see?" he asked.

"Are there live model classes here?" Lana asked.

"Yep, I take it you're into art?"

"Kind of," she said, looking up. He had bright blue eyes and dark brown hair, his jawline chiseled. She had her arms crossed, her fingers playing with the chain around her neck. "Are you one of the instructors?"

He shook his head, "Just a student. Professor Baldwin is wonderful though."

Lana knew that name and smiled, glad her old acquaintance was still teaching.

"What's your name?" he asked.

"Lana, yours?"

"Aiden."

"I'll see you around then," she said, looking back at each canvas. One had the body structure of a young woman with short brown hair and light gray eyes. She sat with her legs tucked beneath her and a dark book of some sort in her hands on her lap. Another was a painting of the young man behind the booth, Aiden, leaning up against a pillar in jeans and a loose-fitting t-shirt. Lana looked back at him, now sitting in the chair focusing his attention on a sketchbook.

Chapter 4

February 7, 1840

"She is breathing normally now, and her fever has gone down," the doctor said. "When she wakes, she will still be very weak."

"Thank you, Dr. Adams. We really appreciate all that you have done for her," Elijah said.

"It was so kind of you to take her in," Dr. Adams said. "You are a fine young man. Your mother would be proud."

Elijah motioned for the housekeeper to escort the doctor out, Abigale watching the girl from beside the window.

"She should be waking up soon," Elijah said, only half-believing his own statement.

"And then we can send her on her way?" Abigale asked.

"She still needs to regain her strength, Abby. She is not going anywhere," he answered.

"You'd like that, wouldn't you? For her to stay?" Abigale said. "She is a distraction, Elijah. Nothing but a damn distraction!"

"Do not raise your voice, you will wake her," he said. "Go for a walk or something, please. You need to calm down."

After Abigale left the room, Elijah sat on the edge of the bed. He wrung water out of a wet cloth, pressing the material lightly to the girl's forehead and then her cheeks. She turned her head toward his hand, opening her eyes slowly.

Startled, she quickly moved away from him, grabbing at the sheets to cover her barely clothed body. All she could do was stare at him as she tried to find her voice but couldn't.

"My name is Elijah. I found you while I was traveling, and you were unconscious. You were very sick and my family took you in," he said.

"Lana," she said softly, her voice cracking.

He moved closer when she backed up against the headboard, trying to keep distance between them.

"Please don't be afraid. I will not harm you," he said, smiling. "What was your name again?"

"My name is Lana," she said again, still cautious about the young man in front of her.

"Do you remember anything?" he asked.

Another man entered the room after knocking briefly. "Eli, I was wondering what you were planning on…"

His statement trailed off as he locked eyes with Lana. Hers were dark gray whereas his were light green.

"I'm sorry for the interruption," he said.

"Micah, this is Lana. And I won't be too much longer," Elijah said. "I'll meet you in the parlor in a few minutes."

Micah didn't take his eyes off Lana as he responded, 'all right' to his brother.

"It was nice to meet you, Lana. I look forward to the day when you have fully recovered."

Lana watched as Micah left the room, and at that moment, she realized she had found people who seemed to care about the wellbeing of a stranger: the man trying to calm her fears of him, the other man wishing her a successful recovery. These were characteristics of people she had been longing to find.

She relaxed a little, lowering the sheets and looking back at Elijah who sat on the bed with her.

"I do not wish that you trust us, but I ask that you give it a thought. You have nothing to fear, Lana. You are welcome here, so please stay as long as you would like," Elijah said.

After that, he placed the rag in the water bowl and exited the room, closing the door behind him.

Lana slid back under the covers, turning onto her side. She thought of what she had considered home and how things had changed so much since she left. For so long, she traveled, thinking she would not find anything close enough to call home again.

As she thought of the kindness the men had shown her, Lana figured she should trust them. They took her in, a stranger they'd never met before, and helped her become healthy again, helped her recover from her illness. Elijah had said she was welcome here, and that alone told her there was hope, hope that she had finally found somewhere to call home again.

~

Lana watched as raindrops pelted her roses while beads of water slid down the glass diligently. A ring dangled from the chain around her neck with a purple gem glistening in the light. Her hair was braided messily, strands of her bangs tucked behind her ear as she leaned her forehead against the window. The glass was cool, a circle of fog under her nose.

She could still see Elijah vividly, his jade eyes in deep sockets, his canines' sharper than any human she'd ever met. She remembered the way his hair fell in his face after a long day of work in the stables, the way he followed Abigale around like a lost puppy. Abigale. Of course, she'd be part of the founding sisters of the university.

A leather-bound journal sat in her lap, her left hand playing with a ribbon meant to keep her place. Lana lifted the cover and fumbled through worn pages until the maroon ribbon loosened from the creases.

Why do I do this to myself?

Her breathing stayed steady as she pictured Professor Thomas pacing back and forth in front of the stage. His story of vampires and his view on whether they were real or not reminded her of the day he confronted her regarding the photo of her and Micah in a frame worn down with age. She could still feel the compression of his hand around her bicep when he grabbed her, could hear his words, his voice begging her for an answer.

Lana ran her left hand up her arm, massaging where Kyle's was that day. Her knees pulled up to her chest, the journal falling to the floor with a thud.

"Hey, I was looking everywhere for you at the festival," Rae said, dropping her folder on the divan across from the window seat. "What happened to you?"

The rain dwindled to mist, rose petals littering the ground around the bushes.

"I didn't feel well."

"You're lying," Rae said, sitting across from her friend. She reached over, tugging on her chin until Lana looked at her.

"Kyle being at the school bugged me," Lana's eyes focused on her fingers intertwining each other. "And then the art booth had a canvas painting of me done by my old art teacher. I thought I could handle coming back, but I don't know if I can."

"I know what you need," Rae smiled. "There's a party tonight at one of the frat houses. That girl from Beta Psi invited us!"

Lana's eyes met Rae's, a light blue ring of light circling her pupil. "Why are your eyes different?"

"This is what happens when I use my powers," Lana said. "I was depressed, and I wanted it to rain."

"Shame on you for playing with the weather," Rae said, slapping Lana's leg. "C'mon, let's get ready."

She heaved Lana off the window seat and closed the curtains. "You really like shaming me."

The girls went upstairs, Lana pulling on a pair of dark skinny jeans and a flowy maroon blouse. She tucked her necklace into the shirt and unbraided her hair, twirling it into a messy bun, tendrils of lavender-colored hair curling around dark brown strands. The blue in her eyes had faded, leaving light circles on her skin beneath them.

Lana rubbed some concealer and foundation on her cheeks to get rid of the circles, lining her eyelid with a light red liner and her black lashes grew a quarter inch with mascara. Rae stood in her doorway once she left the bathroom, grabbing her arm as soon as she got close.

"You've gotta stop that, you're going to make me trip one of these days," Lana laughed.

~

Boys in button-downs and khakis stood on the front porch of a two-story Victorian home holding solo cups filled with questionable liquid and talking up girls dressed in everything from Sunday best to sweats and a t-shirt. Rae and Lana snuck past them until they found Vanessa from orientation.

"Rae! I'm so glad you could make it," she said. She had sun-kissed skin and light brown eyes with shoulder-length black hair. "Lana, it's good to see you again."

"I'm sorry I seemed a little distracted earlier," Lana shook the girl's hand. "It's nice to meet you."

Vanessa guided them to the refreshments where they grabbed drinks and looked around at the desperate college girls looking for a cute frat boy. She pointed out each of the Beta Psi sisters, some of the prospective pledges, as well as those Delta Sigma brothers and their pledges. Rae grabbed the attention of a boy sitting against the wall sipping his drink, Vanessa naming him as Austin. He'd been a student for a year and refused to rush a fraternity but still hung out at the parties.

The girls left Lana at the table to talk with Austin. She poured a drink and looked around, the boy from the art table making his way toward her.

"I guess you were right, I would see you around," he joked, grabbing a cup and pouring a drink from the punch bowl. "Lana, right?"

"Right," she covered her mouth with her cup, sipping at it.

"What brings you out here? Not a lot of freshmen come to these parties," Aiden said, walking toward some bar stools a few feet from the table, Lana following. She took a seat, keeping Rae within eyesight.

"Beta Psi invited my friend who dragged me along," Lana said, watching Vanessa leave Rae with the suspicious boy on the wall. Rae's smile got bigger and bigger as she twirled her hair with her finger.

"Is she the one talking with Austin?" Aiden asked, taking a sip of his drink.

"Yeah, she's a flirt," she huffed. "So, what do you study?"

"History."

"Good for you, we need more historians in this world," Lana said.

"What about you?"

"Psychology and art," Lana said. "I want to help people."

"Good for you, we need more psychologists in this world," Aiden smiled, earning one from Lana. "What did you think of the portraits on my booth today?"

"I thought they were very well done and that they deserved to be hung in a gallery," Lana made a rainbow with her hand as if wiping away Windex on a window.

"You're lying," Aiden said. "Honestly, as an art major you're to analyze and critique."

She looked at him, his eyes a deeper blue than earlier that day. "I recognized one of the pieces from Professor Baldwin when she taught at the high school a few years back. And I also saw the one of you."

"And?"

"They need work," Lana said, looking back where Rae had been standing. She saw the cups the two had been drinking from on the stairwell banister. "I'll be right back."

She set her drink on the bar and scooted the stool underneath before turning from Aiden and heading up the stairs. At the top, an oval mirror and entryway table forced her to go left. Doors on either side of the hall were closed, lights either on or off. The end of the hall turned right, another set of doors on either side yet the only open one was the one straight ahead, no lights on.

Lana peaked her head into the room, the shadow of a man all she could see lying on the bed. She flicked the light switch, what she thought was Austin rearing his head back to see her. His eyes were pitch black, his hand holding Rae's head back so her throat was completely exposed. He launched himself off

28

the bed, knocking Lana into the door, the hinges breaking at their combined weight. Austin stretched his mouth wide, revealing razor sharp teeth and tar dripping from the roof of his mouth. Lana pushed him away, the overwhelming smell of rotting garbage sickened her, her eyes watered.

Aiden slid around the corner, the black figure hunched on the other side of the doorway. He spun a small dagger around in his hand ready to launch when the figure stood, his eyes locked on Aiden. When Austin charged, Aiden sunk the dagger into his abdomen. He disappeared in a cloud of black smoke. He was by her side, heaving her from the ground and leading her to the bed next to Rae.

"What happened?" they asked simultaneously.

"Not sure, but he's gone," Aiden said. "I'm gonna go talk to Lance and I'll be right back."

After he left, Lana and Rae looked around the room for an alternate exit. The window behind the bed slid open without a sound, Lana's blouse clinging to her skin. She slipped through it, her feet barely reaching the slanted overhang beneath them. Once steady, Rae followed, sliding the window down as she descended. They hopped off the overhang, following along the side of the house toward the front lawn. Lana's Elantra, parked across the street, came to life when she reached into her pocket and pressed the auto-start button on the key fob.

Back in the hallway, Aiden pulled his phone out of his pocket as he rounded the corner. He dialed the last incoming number, letting it ring.

"Hey D," Aiden said. "You were right."

"We'll get the clubhouse set up," the voice said on the other line. "Call us if anything changes."

~

The cabin was cold as a young man clothed in dark sweats and a white t-shirt knelt by the fire. The tip of a glistening blade poked away at planks of wood feeding the flames.

The floor creaked, followed by another male figure, his hair slicked back with grease, clearing his throat.

"What news have you brought me, Rayaz?" the man at the fire asked.

"Alric has failed, sir," Rayaz said.

As the fireman sighed, he took the scorching metal in his hand, the skin beneath the blade sizzling like bacon.

"Do you know why I endure this pain, Rayaz?"

The man shook his head. "I am not sure, sir."

"Inflicting pain to myself helps me keep my mind off inflicting pain on my subjects," he said as he stood, facing the man in the doorway. "I could harm you Rayaz, but I fear that if I do, then no other person will be capable of leading me where I need to go."

"I do not mean to insult, Mr. Donovan. But why can you not go there yourself? Clover Bay is not enchanted. It is not protected," Rayaz said.

"Innocents do not deserve to die because of a hunch," Donovan said, glossy eyes reflecting ember flames as he spoke.

"Sir, you are speaking in riddles," Rayaz whispered.

"I cannot return to Clover Bay until I am certain that I have a reason to," he said.

"What reason would that be, Donovan?" Rayaz asked.

"You know me, give me one."

~

"What was he?" Rae asked as Lana drove home.

"He was a member of the Darkness," Lana said, rubbing her neck. "I thought it was odd how quickly he drew you in and then when you disappeared, I knew something was wrong."

"Who was that guy too?"

"He's a history major," Lana said. "I guess he followed me but I don't think he saw anything."

Once the car was secured in the garage, Lana and Rae entered the home, Lana checking each door three times to ensure they were locked. She met Rae in the kitchen, putting a kettle of water on the stove for tea.

"Chamomile will help us sleep," Lana said, taking two cups from the cabinet above the sink to the left.

"Can I have a double dose?" Rae joked, running her hands through her hair. "Lana, don't lie to me."

"Where is that coming from?" Lana turned toward Rae, setting the cups on the counter.

"It's time you tell me everything, from the beginning," Rae said. "I need to know what you are, why you're here, who Kyle is and what we're up against. You can't keep me in the dark forever."

Lana's cell phone rang, Rae sliding off her seat, her stilettos clicking the tile as she paced. Caller ID showed *Dimitri* was calling.

"Are you alright?" Dimitri asked.

"I'm fine," she said, the kettle on the stove whistling. "There's going to be an attack in a week. I'll call if there are any others."

"Please do," he said, ending the call.

Lana grabbed the kettle from the stove and poured two cups of tea before putting it back. She handed one to Rae after the Seer took back her seat.

She took a deep breath, "It all started here in 1840."

Chapter 5

Lana told Rae about the day she woke in the Jacobs' manor after having recovered from a severe illness that should have killed her had she been human. There she met Elijah and his brother Micah, as well as Beta Psi's founding sister, Abigale Jenkins. Lana spent six months on the Jacobs' property being wooed by Micah. She spent a birthday by his side and Abigale continued to loathe her and the fact she came into their lives when she did. Abigale was cordial in public but they never saw eye to eye when they were alone.

Micah and Abigale were walking out at the pastures when Lana saw them together, and Abigale put her plan into motion. All Lana saw was the two kissing, and the rest was a blur. She remembered running, running past the gazebo and barn, through the pastures and into the woods, the woods which local authorities had been patrolling constantly trying to capture the 'animal' that had been taking the lives of citizens in the Bay. Elijah had chased after her without her knowledge.

Not long after Lana had made it into the woods was she confronted by the patrol, only it was not a friendly confrontation. His bayonet tore through her abdomen, knocking the air from her lungs. She lay bleeding on the forest floor when Elijah found her, as did Dimitri, but she didn't wake in the forest.

Dimitri had taken her from the Bay to a safe place, she said. There, he told her what she was, and what her purpose as the type of Fury she was would be. He also told her she would be starting her training as soon as she recovered.

"He said that I was the Amethyst Fury, and the others were Ruby, Emerald, Sapphire, and Diamond," Lana said. "But we were only referred to these names in text books, scrolls written by the Elders. I was so confused. I didn't want to be there, I just wanted to be dead. I begged him to kill me."

Dimitri had continued, dismissing her desire to die. He told her each of the other Furies' names corresponded with what their elemental power was. Ruby controlled the element of Fire, Emerald the element of Earth, Sapphire controlled Water, and Diamond controlled Wind. Together, these four Furies would train her, the Amethyst or Light Fury, to control each of their respective elements and that once she learned to control these elements, she could control Light.

"My destiny is to destroy the Darkness," Lana said, staring into her cup of tea.

"Why is it *your* destiny? There aren't any other Light Furies?" Rae asked, leaning forward.

"There can only be one Fury of each element at a time," Lana said. "When one Fury dies, another is born."

"But that doesn't answer my other questions," Rae said, leaning on the counter. "Why can't you be back here? After all these years, those people aren't here anymore. And Kyle is just one guy. You sure know how to hold a grudge."

"Rae, I'm tired," Lana scratched her head, tucking her bangs behind her ear. "Can we talk about this more in the morning?"

"Sure, whatever," Rae said, chugging the rest of her now cold tea. "It's not like we're running out of time or anything."

"Where are you going?" Lana called after her.

Rae turned, placing both hands on the doorframe. "I think I'm going to stay with my parents tonight."

Lana watched as Rae picked up her folder from the divan, followed by hearing the front door slam shut.

Chapter 6

The streets of Clover Bay were quiet as she walked past The Hideout and the real estate agency, the young woman stopping in front of the spice shop. The grandfather clock in the left-hand corner chimed three times – 3 a.m.

"I didn't expect to see you again," he said, his hands in the pockets of a hooded sweatshirt. "What brings you back here?"

"You always said this was my home," she said, turning to face him.

"It has been for some time." He looked over his shoulder, rocking back and forth onto his heels. "Lana…"

"It was me in the photo," she exhaled. "What do you want from me, Kyle?"

"The same thing you want from me," he said. "Answers."

The two entered the spice shop, the man locking it behind him. "I guess you want to know who I am and I you. And why you were here in the first place."

"I guess I should just gather all the magical beings in the land and sit them down for story time!" Lana clapped her hands together, a nervous laugh on her tongue. "Demon hunter, I already know what you are."

"That's funny, Lana," Kyle laughed. "Josephine told you when you left, didn't she?"

Lana nodded, leaning against the sales counter. "Yet she failed to tell me what you are. What a friend she is."

"I'm tired of story time. Do I really have to tell you the nuts and guts?" Lana crossed her arms. "I'm a Fury. I found my way here, fell in love, yadda, yadda."

"And then the vampires scared you off," Kyle stepped closer.

"More like betrayed me," Lana said, staring at the clock. "Six months of loyalty to that family and Abigale…"

"Why did you leave me?" Kyle's face was inches from her, his eyes staring into hers as if hypnotized. "I would have accepted you, protected you."

Lana's hands met his chest, pushing him away but he failed to move. "Why are you doing this?"

"I just need to know why you left," Kyle said. His hands wrapped around her wrists, his nails digging into her skin.

Tears streamed from her eyes, "Kyle, you're hurting me!" Lana screamed, a gust of wind sweeping him off his feet. Landing on his back a few feet from her, Lana hopped over him, her nervous hands fumbling the lock on the door.

"You shouldn't have done that, Lana," Kyle said, pushing himself off the floor.

The lock clicked, Lana jerking the door open. She slammed it behind her, sprinting down the street toward the university, Kyle in tow. Her feet pounded the sidewalk, the cobblestone streets. Strands of hair stuck to her cheeks sticky from tears.

"Lana, why are you running?" Kyle yelled after her. "We can talk about this."

She didn't look back as she stepped up onto the grass leading to the common area of the school, heading toward a group of men near the fountain.

"Help, somebody help!" Lana yelled, running into a man in a leather jacket and dark jeans. He turned around, his hair slicked back. He caught her as she stumbled. "He's after me. He's going to hurt me."

She looked back, Kyle nowhere to be found.

"He was right there," she pointed weakly, her breathing heavy. Her hair fell around her face, the man tucking it behind her ear.

"It's okay, you're going to be okay," he said. Lana recognized his voice, its soft, almost melodic tone. She looked back at him, her eyes meeting his.

"Elijah?" she asked before everything went black. She came to sit in a small Sedan, the smell of sweat and pine lingering in the air. Thick trees blurred past as Elijah drove down bumpy backroads.

April 10, 1840

"Micah, where are we going?" Lana asked. She gripped the hems of her skirts as they ran through fields of knee-high grass and wildflowers.

A youthful man with black hair laughed and spun around until he was facing her. His light green eyes locked with hers while he attempted to catch his breath. Being breathless in her presence was a common occurrence when he looked at her.

"Have I told you how magnificent you look today?" Micah said, taking her hand.

Her smile was blinding as small rosy spheres dotted her cheeks. She had light gray eyes that grew brighter when she was with him, and brown ringlets fell around her shoulders as they came unpinned. Violet was a color Micah found fit her well, with a hint of white lace and ribbon down her back.

"We better hurry if we are to make it on time," he said, pecking her cheek before running off toward the trees.

"Micah, the forest," Lana said softly.

"No one will hurt you, Lana, not while I'm alive." Micah took hold of her hand and pulled her toward the forest.

They searched for a path for hours until they made their way to a white-boarded monastery on the edge of town. A pointed roof with a white cross decorated the church while patrons of the evening service opened brown wooden doors.

"Just in time," Micah whispered, out of breath from running.

"Do you always take the long way 'round, Mr. Jacobs?" Lana asked, lacing her fingers in his. Her hand was cool despite running through the trees while he looked her over once more.

"Well, Miss McDowall, I'll leave that to your imagination," he smiled. They walked toward the stairs as the people started to blur.

~

Lana's name was called, sounding distant, like a whisper in the wind, fading with the memory.

"Lana," Elijah said, shaking the woman beside him.

She lay on a leather couch worn down over the years with cracks in the material and a down pillow beneath her head. She looked around the room, the white walls coming into view. She recognized the room immediately as she sat up and placed her feet on the ground. Elijah had taken off her jacket and laid her down.

Across from her, a large dark brick fireplace sat against the wall with old photos of men and women she remembered from a time far away in her mind on its mantel. Lana breathed in the musty smell of a home that had been vacant for many years.

"Why did you bring us here?" she asked, her eyes swelling with tears.

"I had to make sure he didn't follow us. After what you experienced, it was the only way I could ensure nothing else happened to you," his voice was soft as he spoke, something she admired about him. "What were you dreaming about?

"About your unconventional routes," Lana joked, looking back around the room once more.

"About Micah's," Elijah said.

He knew Lana didn't want to admit having thoughts of his brother, knew she'd rather forget him altogether.

"You said his name."

Lana leaned into the couch, wiping away her tears with the backs of her hands.

"I know you probably have questions for me," Elijah said as he took a seat beside her, his hands clasped in front of him. "But first, who was chasing you?"

She pulled her knees under her and faced him, her arms crossed her chest. "His name is Kyle. A few years ago, I came back to town and he and I were together. But as a historian, he was able to dig up photos of me and Micah."

"How? The only photos of the two of you are in this house," Elijah said.

Lana ran her left hand over her upper right arm. "Kyle was working on a restoration project with the historical society to preserve the house. He invited me out one day and met me at the gazebo. He showed me the photo and I panicked."

Elijah kept two feet of distance between them, unsure how an attempt at comfort would go over. "And you left town?"

Lana nodded, running her index finger under her eyes. "Is it my turn to ask you questions?"

"Yes…" he said.

"What are you?"

"I'm a vampire," he said calmly. "Abigale turned us after you left."

"Us…" she whispered.

"Micah and I." He stood and paced the length of the fireplace, his hands in his pockets. "The patrolman who found you in the woods, he and the rest of the patrols gathered Abigale and Leah, along with others whom they had turned over the years in the Bay, and burned them in the cellar under the old church. When we confronted them, they took us down. I found myself crawling out of a shallow grave near the barn…"

"I knew I needed to feed if I wanted to live," Elijah continued. "Live…what a wonderful way to live."

"At least you had the option," Lana mumbled.

"Why did you come back here?"

"God, Elijah. You too? Why is everyone so obsessed with why I'm here?" Lana asked, rising to meet him at the fireplace. "What about me is so enthralling that everyone just has to know?"

"Kyle chasing you, the frat party earlier."

"You know about that?" Lana took a step back.

"I was there," he closed the gap. "The people who care about you are worried."

"Oh yeah, all two of them," she stated.

"You forgot about me," Elijah said.

"Until tonight, I didn't even know you still existed, yet you seem to know and be comfortable with the fact that I still do too."

"Dimitri has remained in contact with me since you left the Bay," Elijah put his hands on his hips. "I've watched over you as best as I could without drawing attention to myself for I feared this would happen."

"I don't hate you…"

"But you hate what we are."

Lana had never thought about it that way. Her bitterness toward what she was resulted in a bitterness in anything supernatural, even toward those she once cared deeply for.

"You're probably tired," Elijah changed the subject, tucking a piece of hair behind her ear. "You are safe here, Lana. I promise no harm will come to you in this house. Not while I'm here anyway."

"Micah said that once," she said softly.

She leaned her face into his palm, his thumb running over her soft skin. It had been a long time since he had felt a woman's skin, or at least the skin of someone he was once infatuated with. Had he never been with Abigale, maybe he would have fought with his brother over her.

"Lana, why did you come back?" he asked again.

"I wanted to believe that coming home would give me a chance at being normal," Lana said. "When you…your family took me in, it was the first time in I can't remember how long that I felt like everything was going to be okay. I didn't know what I was, just that I had been alive a long time and I couldn't die. I tried, but something didn't want me to."

Tears streaked her cheeks. "I've done nothing but run since that day, and I thought coming here would somehow change all of that."

"We can't be normal, Lana," Elijah said, wiping away tears with his thumb.

He took her hand once more and escorted her up the winding staircase to a room she never thought she would see again. The bed had a sheer canopy over it, as did the windows with sheer curtains, always letting the light in to signify it was time to wake.

"Will you have a problem sleeping here tonight?" Elijah asked, still in the doorway as she re-examined the room. When she shook her head, he leaned against the doorframe. "I'll just be down the hall if you need me, alright?"

He closed the door behind him, leaving Lana alone to reminisce. The closet, once opened, still had mementos from a time when dresses with petticoats ruled women's fashion. There were dresses the color of blood, olive satin and lavender, as well as pearls and bonnets.

Looking out the window, she saw the barn, a brown, decaying building with the doors swung open and a white splintering gazebo where Micah and Elijah would spend their spare time watching her and the other inhabitants of the Jacobs' mansion enjoy a picnic on the lawn or play croquet, all lit by moonlight.

Lana removed the rubber band in her hair until her curls fell to her waist. She took her hair in her hands, running her fingers through it until she had three pieces and began to braid it. Once finished, she took her place on the bed, remembering the day she woke to Elijah taking care of her after recovering from an illness. She never understood why she would watch people get sick and sometimes recover quickly, unless the plague swept through a village and wiped the population out, whereas she would get sick and take weeks or months to recover until the man who found her in the woods explained how illnesses hit their kind harder than any other being.

Staring at the ceiling, she pulled the thin blankets to her chin and rolled over until she faced the window where she spent countless hours watching the horses run in the pasture beyond the Jacobs' property line.

Images filled her mind as she closed her eyes, images of the dress Micah bought her for the annual ball in the ballroom downstairs; the soft fabric, the lacy bodice, and ruffled skirts that flowed as he twirled her.

Lana could almost smell the food, the champagne on the breath of patrons. She could picture the brothers on the staircase, watching the party from above, picture the dresses, their designs, both conservative and risqué.

The grandfather clock struck twelve as Micah took her by the hand, whispering in her ear. She drifted in and out of consciousness, forgetting Elijah was right down the hall.

Chapter 7

Small spheres of light shone through the window, creating freckles of warmth on her cheek. Elijah stood by the window, jade eyes examining overgrown pastures and tangled barbed wire fences. Set in deep sockets, his eyes looked tired, surrounded by dark skin that faded to nearly translucent at his cheekbones. 150 years ago, time in the once pristine barn and pastures left the Jacobs brothers kissed by the sun's angels.

"You don't sleep," Lana stated, grabbing his attention. He shook his head, still leaning against the frame.

"How did you sleep?" Elijah asked.

"Peacefully actually," she smiled. "What do you have planned for today?"

"Classes start today," he said, crossing his arms.

"What? It's Saturday," Lana tossed the sheets aside, twisting her braid into a bun.

"Lana," his shoes clunked against weathered wood. "You were exhausted and needed your rest. You slept through the weekend."

Lana left the room, nearly stumbling down the staircase. Elijah held out her jacket, opening the door. On the highway headed south into town, the car was quiet except for minimal road noise as tires gripped asphalt. Two miles from the Jacobs' mansion, Elijah pulled into Lana's driveway, a two-story home coming into view.

The cobblestone driveway created a semicircular shape around a patch of land. The land was a shade of dark green with a small garden filled with tulips and roses, specifically red and pink tulips and white roses, her favorite.

A porch wrapped around the mansion that was painted dark brown. A hammock-like seat hung from the awning covering the porch. The wall of the house was created with stones, which formed the first four feet of the wall from the ground. Wooden planks painted light gray formed the rest of the outer wall.

The rest of the land surrounding the front of the house was landscaped beautifully, with sculpted shrubbery lining the stonewall of the house and large trees, pecan, pine, and lavender, scattering the property.

A blue Mercedes sat parked in front of Lana's home, Elijah pulling in behind the vehicle. Lana glanced toward the door to see if anyone was standing on the porch. When she couldn't see anyone, they got out of the car, grabbing her book bag. Closing the door, she noticed the man exiting his vehicle.

Kyle leaned against the Mercedes, his hands in the pockets of his khakis as he looked them up and down. He looked at her with a more intimate look, soft and subtle. His hazel eyes dulled slightly as he pushed himself away from his car. He walked toward her then, slowly and keeping his hands in his pockets. As Elijah put himself between them, Lana looked away, trying to avoid eye contact.

"I'm sorry for what I did, Lana," he said. "I was out of line the other night."

"Is that all?" Elijah asked.

"Elijah Jacobs," Kyle said, his face two inches from Elijah's. "You've really lowered your standards since 1840, Lana."

"Vampires and demon hunters are much more alike than you realize," Elijah said. "You're lucky I didn't track you."

"And I you," the demon hunter lifted his chin.

Kyle's left eye twitched before he grabbed a thin wooden rod from the back of his jeans. Elijah turned and pushed Lana toward the house, the Fury stumbling on cobblestones before finding her balance and sprinting to the front door. Looking behind her, Kyle had the vampire in a chokehold, the rod sticking through his abdomen. He pushed Elijah to the ground as Lana barreled through the door, locking it behind her. She went through the double doors to the right of the foyer, closing them behind her and kneeling on the other side of a long leather couch near the fireplace on the opposite wall of the living room.

The front door slammed shut. "Come out, come out wherever you are."

His black leather shoes scuffed the marble floors beneath him as he looked from left to right. Up the grand staircase would take him to the bedrooms of the McDowall mansion. In front of him, a mirror that rose from halfway up the wall to the ceiling reflected his hazel eyes, blond hair that fell on his face, dark circles beneath his eyes. The doors to the right took him to the living area where he used to sweep Lana off her feet and hold her in his arms on the couch before the fireplace during the cold Bay winter.

Kyle turned the knobs, letting the doors swing open slowly. The room looked as it had before. A dark leather couch sat on the far side of the room in front of a fireplace. The curtains were drawn closed, shielding the view of the garden behind the house. Across from the windows were two divans with a glass coffee table in between them, a vase with white roses in the center of it.

A gust of wind shut the double doors behind him, forcing him to turn around. Taking a step back, he ran into Lana.

Kyle swung, missing Lana as she ducked.

She braced herself against the floor with her hands, kicking him in the stomach with her left foot. She spun then, a long silver rod forming in her hands, a purple jewel-encrusted spiral at its tip. As Lana came around to face him, again the rod came swinging from the ground up, digging into his stomach. She followed through with the swing, the pointed tip of the rod penetrating the skin. A liquid darker than blood slid down the rod as Lana lifted him up and over her head, slamming him hard onto the ground.

Blood bubbled from the wound as Kyle gasped for air. She stood straight then, staring down at him.

"What a mistake you have made," he struggled to find the words. Elijah kicked the doors in right as Kyle dissolved into a million black dust particles.

He was at her side as she leaned against the table behind the divan, his hands turning her head side to side in search of scratches or bruises.

As she looked in his eyes, Elijah noticed a white glowing ring spinning circles around her pupil. Each element Lana conjured reflected in a glowing circle around her pupil. The gust of wind startling Kyle utilized the element of wind.

"I didn't let him touch me," she said softly. Elijah didn't speak, only continued to look her over. Her hair was still in its bun but tendrils had come lose. The longer they stood there the more the glowing circle diminished until only her gray irises remained, light and tired.

Elijah always admired her beauty, the agelessness of her face and her youthful features. Her hair had always been perfectly curled and pinned up during the day. It cascaded down her back when she would take the pins out. He tried not to watch her as intently as his brother but could not help but be mesmerized by her beauty and the grace she had. At one point in time, he would have believed maybe she was secretly a vampire by the way her beauty was seamless, that she had no flaws in her façade as the myth of those creatures always stated. Immortality seemed to look good on all creatures.

Her cell vibrated in the back pocket of her jeans, Lana fishing it out and reading the caller ID. Rae.

"Where have you been? I've been trying to get ahold of you for days…" Rae's frustration got the best of her as she stuttered.

"I was visiting a friend," Lana said, her voice almost a whisper. "I'll see you in class."

Before Rae could stammer through another sentence, the screen went black. Lana gathered her books and bag from the walkway, tossing them into her car.

"Mind giving me a lift?" the vampire asked, following closely behind her. "My chemistry class starts at 10."

She nodded, sliding into the driver's seat.

Chapter 8

Lana and Elijah parted ways once they arrived at the campus, the vampire heading to the science wing while Lana went to the fine arts department. Across the quad, she noticed Rae talking to Alexa, Beta Psi must really want her friend.

"Lana! We were just talking about you!" Alexa said, manicured hands on her hips. "Where did you disappear to Friday night? Rae said you two headed out early?"

"We hadn't set up our apartment yet," Rae beat Lana. "She just moved back last week, so we wanted to get settled in before classes started."

Alexa looked Lana up and down. Her hair was greasy under the beret she tucked the mess under in a hurry. The blouse she'd worn to the party bunched up and folded as if she'd slept in it all weekend. News flash…

"Well, I'll let you two go," Alexa said. "Classes start in 10."

"Thanks for covering," Lana said as she and Rae walked toward Malcolm Hall. Each of the buildings at Clover Bay University represented one of the town's founding fathers. Bridger Malcolm was the Bay's first lawyer and led the search party during the vampire infestation.

"Anytime," Rae's voice was low. "I've gotta head to psych. I'll see you at home."

The Seer unlinked arms and dashed in the opposite direction, avoiding eye contact with Lana.

Outside the art building, Aiden leaned against a pillar, a lightly tanned brunette talking his ear off. From the side she looked like Alexa, only her hair had been curled messily and framed her face.

Aiden looked in Lana's direction, the Chatty Cathy following his gaze.

Her feet ceased, her breath catching in her throat. A chill ran up her spine, the hairs on the back of her neck standing straight. Bumps rose on her arms.

The girl had hazel eyes and thin lips, her cheekbones defined like Aiden's. Her nose slanted slightly with a small round tip.

Perfection.

The girl grabbed Aiden's chin in her hand, refocusing his attention on her. Passing them, Lana walked swiftly up the stairs into the building.

"See you after class, Aiden," the girl said, patting his chest before turning on her stilettos.

The art room was divided into sections by various furniture. Long counters on which sat six artists, three on each side, adorned the right side of the room. In the center, stools and easels formed a semi-circle around a 10-by-10-foot stage. A projector hung from the ceiling with a screen behind the platform. On the left of the room, cabinets with nametags and empty frames covered the wall.

Lana took the stool in the center closest to the exit, a mere four rows away from the stage which sat an additional stool. Art was like science to her, she enjoyed discovering new techniques and testing the limits of her ability with different models and subject matter. Live models were particularly challenging because they rarely stood still. She gazed around the room, sizing each student up to determine who would be the model of the day.

Josephine Baldwin, the art professor, stepped onto the platform, placing her thin-rimmed reading glasses on her head. Her blonde curls were pulled into a low pony, short ringlets curled around her ears. Ms. Baldwin looked older than the last time Lana saw her, wrinkles spiking from the sides of her light hazel eyes.

"Good morning students, and welcome to Malcolm Hall," the professor said. "My name is Josephine Baldwin and I will be your instructor for the duration of the semester. My class is unlike any art class you have taken in the past. In fact, it is so different, we do not cover what types of brushes there are, what they do, and how you should properly use them to get a desired effect. Instead, I assign projects from the beginning of the semester and allow you as the artist to interpret said assignment in a way you see fit and critique over time."

A short blonde girl whose feet dangled six inches from the floor sat in the row ahead of Lana. She raised her hand hesitantly.

"Why? Aren't these classes supposed to teach us how to become an artist?"

Professor Baldwin looked toward Lana, "what class are you in?"

"Life Drawing," Lana said softly. The professor nodded.

"And in Life Drawing, we draw just that," she added. "Today, you will be drawing Mr. Morrison."

Aiden emerged from behind a separator wearing only lose fitting jeans. His short brown hair formed into a faux hawk, and he wore a cocky grin as the female students took his figure in.

He had toned abdominal muscles that formed a V shape, disappearing under his jeans, his biceps toned when he flexed. Aiden laughed and Lana could notice his smile was extremely white and beautiful, and how his eyes glistened a little when he did so.

"Your assignment is to take Aiden and create the ultimate fantasy. Yes, he is strikingly attractive, and half dressed, but everyone has a different interpretation of how he looks. I want you all to try and put that interpretation down on paper," she said.

Lana already knew what she would focus on. The center of interest was his face, the high, defined cheekbones and the dimples that appeared when he smiled a little. She would define him by his facial features, not by the body that he probably spent hours in the gym to obtain. In her mind, he was the ultimate male fantasy. He was attractive, his body was very athletic and toned, and he had the eyes that could melt a heart with one glance.

She imagined his hair without all the gel he used, and how he would look with facial hair. Whenever she finished with his hair, she worked on his lips and the smirk that he had given when he walked out. She tried two different angles, an angle from the side and one head-on.

As she glanced at him once more for the final facial detail, his eyes, she caught him staring at her. He had crossed his arms, and bent over more to cover his torso as an obstacle for each student to overcome. He grinned and she looked away, focusing on the eyes in her sketch of him.

She continued to sneak a glance here and there over the edge of her easel, her gray eyes meeting his blue crystal gaze each time. They stared at each other for a minute before Professor Baldwin started speaking.

"All right, time is up," she said, snapping her fingers. She stood up on the platform with Aiden after handing him a shirt to put on. "Now if everyone would please turn their creations around to the front so that we can evaluate them."

Students hesitantly turned their easel around. Some of the first drawings had him lying on his side with his head propped up by his hand leaning on his elbow.

The scene from *Titanic* popped into her head.

He was wearing nothing and had a feather blanket covering his hips, a scene straight off the cover of a steamy romance novel. He had long flowing hair and a look of beckoning in his eyes.

The next had him dressed in a football uniform and a helmet in his hands. He looked exactly as he did now only fully clothed. Lana was the last person to be evaluated, only because she hadn't turned hers around until asked by Professor Baldwin.

Both she and Aiden stepped closer to examine the artwork. She had focused on his face, and not the temptation of drawing him naked like most of the other girls in the class. For this, her instructor commended her.

Aiden watched her as she looked over her own sketch. She explained to the class that she felt the body didn't define the man, that instead the face and, more importantly, the eyes are the first things that are noticed, at least for her.

"The ultimate fantasy doesn't exist," Lana said. "If anything, reality is more obtainable than fantasy, because it is just that. Fantasy. If you had asked me to go off with something fictional, had not put a model in front of me, I would draw him. Or someone that looked almost identical to him. There is no fantasy about him as the model because he is the reality."

"Well done," Professor Baldwin said.

This is why your artwork has always been an example I have used during lessons like these, Lana heard inside her head. She smiled at her instructor and turned her sketch back around.

Aiden was waiting for her, leaning up against a pillar in the garden, when she left the art room.

"That was very impressive," he said. His voice was deep and smooth.

"Thank you," Lana said, keeping her back to him, her head hung low.

"Hey, wait up," Aiden said, touching her arm. "I didn't see you after that issue with Austin after the party."

"Yeah, Rae and I left right away. She was pretty spooked."

"Are you alright?"

She looked up then, "yeah, I'm fine. Just tired. I'll see you around."

Dark circles, the color of bruises formed under her eyes, small raised bumps on her chin. She stuffed her sketchbook in her book bag and headed to chemistry.

It wasn't like Aiden to take to new people, especially women. Christine was around only because she had to be, not because he wanted her to. He'd been alive for a long time, 500 years or so, he lost count. But there was something about Lana… Could it be that she didn't respond like most women to his charm? Maybe it was that she wasn't perfect, that she didn't try to conceal the flaws on her skin like Christine did.

Whatever it was, he had to know.

It could just be that he had saved her life, destroyed that demon who had harmed her and her friend at the party. Maybe he felt he needed to continue to protect her, she should at least expect that's why he's being so nice.

Aiden shook his head. She's just a girl. Just a human. Even if she fell for him, if he let her into his twisted, demented life, he couldn't take her with him, couldn't live happily ever after. She'd die in sixty years, unless she had cancer, and he couldn't cure that. And that's if she believed in magic, if she was fine with the fact that the man she fell in love with has killed people and can't be killed.

Well, he can be.

Stop. Just stop. Christine understands, just stick with her.

Chapter 9

In the quad, Lana braced her back against a tree, a leather-bound journal in her lap. She pulled at the maroon ribbon until it revealed her place and unsheathed the pen from its holster.

It's like I never left, or rather she never died. Elijah said Abigale was burned when the patrol took her, but now I'm not so sure she's really gone.

That girl.
The skin.
Eyes.
Even her stare.
I need to know.

"What do you need to know?" Elijah appeared over her shoulder, reading as she wrote.

"A little privacy here..." Lana laughed, replacing the ribbon and returning the journal to her book bag.

"How was your first class?" he asked, taking a seat across from her.

"It went well," she paused. "I saw this girl outside the building. It could have just been the light, or stress, but she looked so familiar."

"How so?" Elijah asked. He leaned in, his voice. "I think we're seeing the same girl."

"You've seen Abby too?" Lana leaned forward.

He closed his eyes, exhaled, and dropped his head.

"I thought she died…"

"I did too," Elijah said. "But it could be someone else, maybe a relative?"

"She was a vampire, Eli," Lana said. "Unless she had a kid before she was turned."

"She never said anything like that," Elijah said. "Either way, we should assume she's not until we know for sure."

"Not what?"

"Not Abby," Elijah said, his jade eyes meeting hers. "The last thing you need is to be worried about a doppelganger."

Lana fidgeted with her hands, her nails tracing her cuticles.

The thin figure of a teenager approached, her hair pulled back in a high pony. Elijah stood, Lana's head craning back like on hinges.

"You must be Rachel," he said, a smirk on his lips.

"It's Rae, actually," the Seer snarked. Looking down at Lana, Rae ignored Elijah's handshake. "C'mon, it's time for history."

She held out her hand, hoisting Lana from the ground. "But I don't wanna go…"

Elijah snickered, "You never liked history."

"Lana, who is this guy?" Rae gestured with her thumb.

"Rae, this is Elijah," Lana said. "Elijah Jacobs."

Rae dropped her arm, staring him up and down. "You're a bit unattractive for a vampire."

Lana pulled her friend by her bag, the girl nearly tripping. "Now you know how it feels. Rae, how could you?"

"What? I thought vampires were supposed to be beautiful? He was kind of meh," Rae said, pulling her bag from Lana's grip. "How was your class?"

"Whatever," Lana crossed her arms. "Elijah wouldn't date you anyway."

Rae huffed, her feet pounding the gravel sidewalk.

"And you want me to protect her?" Elijah laughed. "She's so not worth it."

"You just have to get to know her. She's really not that bad," Lana smiled. "You fell for Abigale."

Elijah stood still. "And you fell for Micah. I'll see you around, Lana."

"Eli, I didn't mean it like that," Lana called after him. Elijah disappeared in a crowd of bodies.

Chapter 10

Aiden sat on the steps of the Jacobs Library listening to Christine drone on and on about how she wasn't invited to the Beta Psi party, his eyes concentrating on Lana and Elijah.

"I just don't understand what it is about those other new girls that Alexa and Vanessa like," Christine stated. "I mean, look at that one girl Alexa was talking to. Her hair was a mess, she slept in whatever she wore. Like seriously?"

She ran her fingers through her hair, the curls loosening. "Do you think I'm pretty?"

"What?" Aiden's voice was low.

"Are you even paying attention to me?" she put her hands on her hips.

"No," he shook his head.

Her hand met his arm, heaving him from his position. "Why the hell not?"

"Because it's the same thing over and over, Christine. Oh, nobody likes me, boo hoo hoo," Aiden said. "Grow up."

Aiden hopped the remaining four steps, landing softly on the balls of his feet.

Christine dug her nails into the back of her neck, gasping for air. "Aiden, something's wrong."

"It's just a vision," he said, taking the steps two at a time.

"No, it's burning!" the air caught in her throat.

She leaned against him, Aiden pulling her to the ground. "What do you see?"

The pain dissipated, a numbness washing over her. "It's too hard to make out… There were screams. Fire. Do you think maybe it's the attack Dimitri warned about?"

"I don't know," he said. "Go home. I'll see you after class."

~

In her dorm, Christine drew the curtains, darkness encasing the small space. The twin bed was made with a wool blanket and white sheets, all folded under with hospital corners. On the desk across from the bed, books were organized based on size with plain bookends propping them upright.

The chair made a small thud when she placed it on the ground, taking a seat and pulling out the first book in line. Each page described a piece of her childhood. The day her father killed her golden retriever she received her first vision.

She was five.

White and gray Daisy and Dandelion wildflowers wave in the wind as a little girl in a dark gray dress runs her hands over the small flowers. Her white sandals stomp over patches of the fruity-smelling weeds before she bends down to pick a Daisy here and a Dandelion there. Once her tiny hands are full, she races a golden retriever back to the front porch of a shack on the edge of the woods.

A young woman with dark hair and gray eyes turns while the little girl keeps running toward her, holding up her treasure above her head. When the woman kneels to greet her, the little girl stops two feet from the woman, squinting her eyes shut.

The little girl drops the flowers, and sees the golden retriever running in the field, sees her trailing behind the furry friend. The next thing she sees, a small dark blotch getting larger quickly and the dog with its eyes closed. The flowers fall from her hands before she opens her eyes. The young woman has her against her chest, her left hand on her head, her left arm wrapped around the little girl.

Eight years later, the next page read.

A young girl sits at a white table, various drawings scattered across its surface. In one drawing, small hands hold wildflowers, in the next, the flowers lay crumbled on the dirt. Her hair is pulled back in a long braid down her back, the rings on the cuffs of her white jacket tap against the surface of the table as she colors a red splotch on the torso of an animal. She stops coloring briefly. She closes her eyes, the creases on her forehead she never forgets.

The young girl sees an arm with an open hand, the palm facing up. Blood runs along the underside of the arm, dripping on the ground. She sees light reflect from an object on a finger, and moves closer, soon realizing what she has seen.

Once the pain subsides, the girl opens her eyes, a flashing light and siren going off in the room. Two men in white coats grab either arm, putting them behind her back. They place a combination lock through both rings on either cuff of the jacket, locking her arms behind her back. She thrashes, manages to hit one of the men in the face with the back of her head.

Christine flipped through the remaining pages, her hair blowing in the breeze.

"It happened again today," she said softly as she wrote. "The Furies are in danger. All I see are shadows."

The pen clicked before it slid into the pen jar, clinking on the glass bottom. "They would kill me if they saw the tense change."

The sun-kissed brunette let the diary close slowly, reading bits and pieces of her past as each page fanned. The day of her mother's funeral was the first she had been out of the correction facility in eight years. It was also the first day she'd met others like her.

"You may feel as though you are useless, but that is far from the truth," his voice startled her. Dimitri leaned against the edge of the bed, wrinkling the blanket.

"Don't do that!" she cried, pushing him away. "There can't be any wrinkles!"

He grabbed her by the shoulders. "They can't hurt you anymore, Christine."

She brought her hands to her face, her cheeks wet. "Why did you take me away?"

"Nobody deserves to be treated the way you were for being what we are," he said softly. His breath moved the hair by her ear. "Rest, please."

He tugged the covers free, laying the Seer on the bed. "What's going to happen when they come for you?"

"We will destroy them," Dimitri stated. "We will not let them win this time."

Chapter 11

The history classroom was empty save for a few students, Lana a few seats from the door. Taking the seat behind her, he noticed the tattoo behind her ear. A Gemini symbol.

"Gemini, huh?" he asked, keeping himself distracted.

"I'm sorry?" Lana looked behind her, slightly confused.

"Your tattoo, it's the Gemini zodiac symbol."

"Oh, yeah," she smiled slightly.

A squirrely looking woman entered the room from the front door, pushing her thin-rimmed glasses up the bridge of her nose.

"Unfortunately, today's lecture has been canceled as Mr. Thomas has unexpectedly quit," her voice shook. "Please do not return to this classroom until you have been notified that the class has been issued an instructor."

The remaining students packed up their things quickly, some nearly running out the door. Aiden took his time, waiting for Lana to finish putting her book in her bag before following her out the door. Although she knew he was following her, she paid no attention to him.

He touched her arm gently, clearing his throat. "I saw you and your boyfriend in the quad earlier, is everything alright?"

"Boyfriend?" she squinted her eyes. "No, he's just a friend. And everything's fine."

"He stormed off…"

"He does that…" Lana crossed her arms. "I have to go."

"Would you like to join me for coffee later?" Aiden called after her, his hands in his pockets.

She turned to him, "Not tonight."

It wasn't like him to question his feelings. Watching her walk away was like a slap to the face, a blow to his ego. Christine fawned over him, and Lana couldn't care less. She kept her head low, eyes to the ground, left hand clasped over the top of her book bag.

Aiden ran his hands through his hair, linking his fingers behind his head.

"Lana," Aiden called after her. "Lana, wait up."

"If you know what's good for you, you will stop following me," Lana said, speeding up her pace. Aiden ran to catch up with her, grabbing her wrist and turning her around.

"Are you deaf?" she said rudely.

"I'm stubborn, there's a difference," Aiden said, smirking.

Lana attempted to avoid eye contact, crossing her arms and diverting her gaze to a tree in the quad.

He tilted his head slightly, realizing how much more tired she looked. Her skin was slightly paler and shadows had appeared under her eyes.

"Let me walk you to your car, please," Aiden said.

He half-expected a no. She sighed, turning on her heels. "The Hideout has good coffee. Have you been there?"

Aiden's gait fell in line with hers. "I've had better."

"It's the best Clover Bay has," Lana stated.

"You've been here before?" her nose twitched and a smile grew on her lips at his question. He must have forgotten their conversation the night the Darkness attacked her and Rae at the frat house.

"That surprises you?" she asked, letting go of her book bag.

"I didn't expect it, that's all."

Dimitri leaned against Aiden's truck, watching the two head to her car.

Aiden opened her door, Lana tossing her book bag into the back seat. "I'll see you at the Hideout."

"Who's that?" Dimitri pretended.

"No one," Aiden tugged on the handle.

"Why aren't you with Christine?" he asked as Aiden climbed into the vehicle.

"She had a vision and needed to rest, and I had class," Aiden pulled the door shut.

Dimitri sat in the passenger seat, green haze filling the cabin. "Where are you headed?"

"Seriously, D?" Aiden refused to back out.

"What?" Dimitri fastened the seatbelt. "I haven't seen you in a while. I thought we could catch up."

"I'm busy," Aiden said. "Get out."

"With that girl? What do you know about her?" Dimitri asked. "Is she single? Is she magical? What is she studying? How old is she?"

"I haven't asked," he shook his head. The reality was all he knew about Lana was her major and not much else.

"What do you expect to get out of this coffee date?"

"Go check on Christine."

"Already did. She's asleep."

"Well then, go fuck Terra."

"Watch your language."

"Dimitri, get the hell out of my truck. I have places to be," Aiden stated.

~

Outside the coffee shop, Aiden scanned the street for Lana's car, his hands in his pockets. A slow breeze swept his loose hair, sending a chill down his spine.

"I didn't mean to make you mad earlier," Lana said, her hands cupping her latte.

"Don't worry about it, we all say things we don't mean," Elijah smiled.

Lana lifted her eyes, focusing on the man entering the coffee shop.

"Mind if I join you guys?" Aiden asked.

"Sure, I was just leaving," the Vampire said. "Aiden, right?"

"Yeah," the two shook hands, Elijah's skin cold. Aiden hated vampires.

"I'll call you later, Lana," Elijah waved, tossing his coat on when he got outside.

"So how did you two meet?" Aiden asked, Lana sipping her drink.

"We met a few years ago on a restoration project of the Jacobs' manor," Lana said.

"Is he related to the family in any way?" he asked. "That'd be cool if he was. That family was pretty twisted."

"Great, great grandson I think. Maybe there's another great in there, I'm not sure," she sipped her latte, the caramel aroma filling her nostrils.

"Do you believe in the supernatural?" Aiden shot straight to the point.

Lana set her cup down, pondering the question. An odd question to ask someone he'd just met, she kept her eyes on the foam slowly dwindling to a few white bubbles on top of the liquid.

"Do you?" her gray eyes met his. He turned his head, biting his lip before speaking.

"I do. I believe things happen for a reason, sometimes unexplainable things and when things cannot be explained by science, I tend to lean toward the supernatural meaning or occurrence of things," Aiden said. "You didn't answer my question."

"So, you're saying you believe vampires really did attack Clover Bay over 100 years ago and that it wasn't random animal attacks that killed those hikers…" Lana stated.

"That's correct," Aiden crossed his arms, leaning against the table. "And just between you and me," he lowered his voice, "I don't think your friend is as distantly related to the Jacobs' as he's letting you believe."

"Is that so?"

"You still haven't answered my question, Lana," he asked once more.

"I think that you're crazy, and that you should stay away from me," she grabbed her bag, swinging it over her shoulder. On her way out the door, she stopped, staring straight through the window at a familiar figure.

"Lana?" Aiden saw nothing.

She left the coffee shop, tossing the bag by the rear tire of her car before sprinting after the figure. Aiden chased her through busy sidewalks and across the street toward Clover Bay Cemetery.

The wrought iron gates were locked, Lana pulling at the thick, rusted lock and chain.

"What is going on?" Aiden put his hands on his knees, pretending to be out of breath. "Were you in track or something?"

"Or something," Lana said, looking for handholds in the swirled design of the gate. Once she found them, she began scaling the gate, placing each foot where each hand was previously and pushing to the next available handhold. Aiden watched as she swung her body over, clashing against the other side and nearly losing her grip.

When she was about five feet from the ground, Lana leapt from the gate, the hard landing sending a shock of pain through her knees. Aiden backed up, running toward the gate. He scaled it in less time, swinging his body over the gate gracefully and releasing his hands from the iron. He landed softly on the balls of his feet, fingertips lightly touching the dirt beneath him.

Lana saw from the corner of her eye but disregarded him, scanning the cemetery for Kyle.

"Oh c'mon, you can't say you weren't impressed by that," Aiden leaned back slightly, his hands out to his side, palms facing the sky.

"I wasn't," she said softly. They walked a few paces into the cemetery before hearing clapping behind them.

"Bravo, bravo," Kyle said, slow clapping. "That was impressive to me, Aiden."

"Professor Thomas," Aiden said. "Why are you hanging out in a cemetery?"

"I could ask you the same thing, but you should ask her," he pointed at Lana who positioned herself behind Aiden. "Aw, look at that, already hiding behind you."

"You two know each other?"

"Knew," Kyle corrected the Fury. "But I'm sure if you asked her, she'd deny everything."

"That's not true," Lana said.

"It's not? Huh, well that's good, I guess," Kyle sighed. "How was your coffee date? Talk about anything good?"

"Why do you care?" Aiden asked.

"Isn't it obvious? I still care about her and you're trying to take her from me," Kyle exclaimed. "God, you're dense."

Lana took a step back, making sure to stay exactly behind Aiden.

"You really think she won't do the same to you?"

"And what exactly will she do?"

"Leave without any explanation," Kyle said. "Just up and leave you with questions about why and what you did wrong... Kind of like that."

Lana hurdled the stone casing before sprinting through the cemetery toward the back entrance.

"Bet I can catch her before you," Kyle taunted, turning and scaling the gate.

Once they were both out of sight, Aiden disappeared in a red haze, appearing in an alley close to her vehicle. Kyle was there shortly after, Elijah pushing him into the wall.

"I thought I told you to leave Lana alone," Elijah said, his fangs dropping from his gums.

Kyle's laugh was deep and menacing. "You can't kill me, vampire. It doesn't work that way."

He waved goodbye, disappearing quickly. Elijah fell forward, bracing himself against the wall.

Aiden crossed the street, meeting Lana at the corner of the building. He opened the back door of his truck for her, helping her inside. They left the city, leaving Elijah behind to deal with the demon hunter.

Chapter 12

Lana was quiet, Aiden watching her in the rearview. She'd killed him in her house, the day he tried killing Elijah. He should never have come back. Unless that's not how to kill a demon hunter.

"Are you alright?" Aiden asked.

She remained silent as they drove, unsure where Aiden would take her but glad to be away from the city.

"Take a left here," Lana said when they approached Clover Lane, the road to her home. She didn't care if he knew where she lived, he didn't seem like the type who would stalk her.

A mile into the road her home came into view, Aiden pulling into the driveway. Elijah had driven her car home for her and was waiting in the driveway. The truck came to a stop a few feet behind the car, Lana hopping down from the truck.

She pushed past Elijah, Aiden stopping in front of him.

"Thank you for bringing her home," Elijah said.

"No problem," Aiden said, taking his hand. They stared at each other for a moment before he spoke again. "How do you do it?"

"I'm sorry?" Elijah asked, dropping the handshake.

Aiden's eyes glanced at the door, closed off from the conversation. "How can you be around her? She's perfect, and

I can't begin to imagine what her blood must smell like to you."

Elijah dropped his head, kicking at loose stones on the driveway. "It isn't easy, but she's my best friend. I would never do anything to hurt her. Besides," he looked up. "I eat animals."

"That's not healthy," Aiden said.

"But it keeps me from eating her," Elijah laughed. "Thanks again. I don't know what happened, and she probably won't tell me, but you probably saved her life today."

~

Lana filled the tub, spilling half a bottle of bubble bath into the water once halfway full. She let the warm water take over, relaxing her body until she was fully submerged. She exhaled the air in her lungs, fighting the urge to return to the surface.

This wasn't her first attempt and it wouldn't be her last as she would survive. She always survived. A few weeks after Dimitri had told her what she was and what her purpose was, she'd gone to the basement where they had taught her how to wield weapons, grabbed the neared dagger and split her arm open, taking the tip of the blade from the beginning of her wrist to the crook of her elbow on both arms. She'd lost a lot of blood, but Dimitri knew somehow and had her wounds treated and bound. They'd healed in twenty-four hours.

A few years later, she found herself on a dock listening to the horns of naval carriers long into the night as they docked and set sail. Lana made her way up the coast until she found a small fishing dock, toting two cinderblocks. She walked out to the edge of the dock, taking a step too far until she was submerged in water, both cinderblocks hanging on her arms like jewelry.

Her feet planted firmly in the soft mud beneath the water the moment her lungs ran out of air. She gasped and gasped until she could gasp no longer. She mistook a blue flash of light for the light at the end of a tunnel, but could not feel the arms of a man wrapping around her small frame, pulling her from the water. She woke in the infirmary once more with Dimitri and Wiley, the Water Fury who found her this time, by her bedside.

By now, she'd lost count of the amount of times she'd attempted suicide. She had jumped off bridges into water with blocks of cinder around her arms, tied herself to train tracks, jumped off abandoned or condemned industrial buildings. She'd even traveled to Chernobyl.

When Elijah entered the house, a banshee's scream deafened him.

To his right, the doors to the living room were closed, smoke rising from beneath them. He bounded up the stairs, taking them two or three at a time, until he was at the top of the staircase. The door to Lana's room was locked, Elijah throwing himself against it. In the bathroom, he saw no one except a bathtub overflowing. She'd left the water on.

"Lana?!" he yelled, looking in the walk-in closet before noticing a dark figure in the bathtub beneath the water.

He reached into the water, his hand cupping behind her neck. He lifted her, repositioning his hands so he could hoist her from the tub. He placed his hands beneath her breasts, the palm of his hand beneath the base of her sternum and began counting as he compressed.

Thirty compressions.

Tilt the head. Pinch the nose.

Two breaths.

Return to 30 compressions.

Breathe.

He completed these three times before she bolted upright, coughing up water. Elijah heaved her to her feet, throwing a robe for her to put on as he pulled her through her room and down the stairs. Lana clenched her teeth at the banshee screams.

"It's coming from the living room," Elijah said. "We need to leave the house."

Lana fought him, kicking the living room doors open. Thick clouds of smoke escaped, Lana and Elijah choking.

Coughing, they dropped to their knees, hoping to have breathable air closer to the ground. Visibility was sparse as they made their way in the direction of the kitchen.

As they got closer to it, Lana started coughing more frequently, the smoke blurring her vision each time she opened her eyes. She tried blinking the tears away as her eyes watered. Stopping near a three-foot tall table with white roses resting in a vase, her coughing became furious as the doors leading to the foyer slammed shut.

Lana put her back against the wall next to the table, covering her ears with the palms of her hands. She tried to take a deep breath, focusing on the smoke. She felt wisps of hair tickle her cheeks, Elijah watching her intently. Smoke began to swirl within the living area, whipping around as tornado-like winds swept in through the fireplace in the right-hand corner of the room.

The tornado-like winds picked at areas of the room, small flames quickly turning into a blaze that jumped from couch to wooden furniture and then to curtains. Lana pushed Elijah in the direction of the door when something grabbed her, pulling her toward the window at the front of the house. The curtain wrapped around her neck, choking her. Elijah was pinned to the wall by the door, unable to move as the living room became engulfed in flames.

Dimitri and the other Furies appeared in a haze, Wiley and EJ, the Wind Fury, creating a storm cloud spanning the length of the ceiling. The cloud rained on the living room, the fire sizzling. Once Lana was free, she and Dimitri disappeared in a green haze, Wiley grabbing Elijah before the storm cloud dissipated.

Chapter 13

From the balcony of the clubhouse, Lana saw a forest of Pine trees encroaching the backyard.

"What did you do to piss off a Holanshee?" Dimitri asked, leaning against the screen door.

"What is that?"

"The thing that attacked you," he stated. "A Holanshee is a demon that uses your own power against you. They are identified by their scream, which is that of a banshee, except they are an invisible demon."

"How do you kill one?" Lana asked, picking at the dead skin around her nails.

"You can't," Dimitri said. "Which means you can't return home until we know for sure it has left."

"I have to warn Rae," Lana turned to face him. "She should be going home soon and when she sees the living room…"

"Wiley is taking care of that," Dimitri said, putting his hands in front of him. He took a few steps toward her before clasping his hands and bringing them to his lips. "I know you're tired, Lana, and I know this weekend has been really difficult for you but you can't keep doing this."

"Doing what?" Lana threw her hands out to the side.

"Suicide is not the answer. All it does is deplete your energy and make you an easier target for the Darkness," Dimitri said.

"Then maybe you should try harder to find the Fire Fury so we can get this over with," Lana said, pushing past him.

"We already have," Dimitri said.

She turned in the doorway, her hand on the handle. "And you're just now telling me this?"

"It's not that," Dimitri sighed. "He's…difficult to work with. He's a lot like you, actually."

"Oh really?"

"He wants to be done with all of this," Dimitri stated. "In fact, he's wanted to be done with this since the Crusade. We haven't seen him since, per his request."

"Does he live here? Have I met him yet?" She stepped away from the door, crossing her arms. "Does he know I exist?"

"Yes," Dimitri said. "But he doesn't know your name."

"Tell him then," Lana said, putting her hands on her hips. "Tell me his name."

"Lana, that's enough," Elijah said from the house. "I'm taking her home."

"She can't go home, we've been over this," Dimitri said over her shoulder.

"Not to her home, to mine," Elijah said. "Let's go."

Lana didn't argue, leaving with Elijah. At the Jacobs' manor, Lana sat in the gazebo the remainder of the night, staring out at the moonlit pastures. She couldn't sleep, afraid she'd see Kyle as a demon. She played with the thought of what demon hunters were capable of. Did they make deals with demons they were meant to kill? Were these deals a way of saving the demon's life? I won't kill you if you take care of this person for me. It's the only way they can die – at the hand of a demon. That's what the Darkness consisted of, they said.

~

February 28, 1840

A slender figure sat on a bench in the gazebo, the black waves of his hair combed back. He wore a white collared shirt unbuttoned at the neck, with loose trousers and suspenders. The black boots he wore were muddy after working in the barn.

He looked out across acres of land; watching horses run through the pasture and cows graze on fresh grass. A woman in a red dress walked along a white picket fence, trailing her finger along the wood. Her dress was made of a satin material, with black lace embroidery and ruffles at the cuffs. Her hair was pulled back in tight curls and she wore a pearl necklace and earrings to match. White gloves covered her hands as she stopped and stared across the pasture at the horses galloping.

"She's recovering at a remarkable rate," Elijah said. The man in the gazebo was startled, looking at the man who interrupted his daydream.

"If you believe three weeks to recover from pneumonia is a quick recovery, something is terribly wrong with you, brother," Micah said.

"Dr. Adams said it was a miracle she survived so regardless of the time, she is recovering. Micah, why are you watching her so intently?"

Micah, caught off-guard by his brother's question, looked at him then. "Keeping an eye on a sick person is not a crime, Elijah."

Elijah laughed, his light green eyes finding the girl in the scarlet dress. "If I'm not mistaken, I would say that you are infatuated with her."

"I'm sorry, but you are mistaken," Micah said. He stood, leaving the gazebo. He looked in the girl's direction but continued walking toward the house.

She continued to stare out toward the horses until Elijah stood beside her.

"You have a very beautiful home," Lana said. "Thank you for helping me."

"It was the right thing to do, ma'am," he said.

"Please, call me Lana."

"May I ask your last name?" Elijah asked.

"McDowall, Lana McDowall," she answered. "And yours?"

"Jacobs," he returned. "It is very nice to meet you formally, Miss McDowall."

~

Elijah's voice woke her up. She was on the floor of the worn-down gazebo, splinters poking at her back.

"Rae is at her parents' house for the time being," he said. "I think you should go there and explain why she can't come home."

"Dimitri said they were taking care of it..." Lana wiped gunk from her eyes.

"She doesn't know about the demon."

She looked over her shoulder at the field, the horses galloping and stopping to graze every now and then. She'd taught Rae how to ride last time she was in the Bay. Rae's family lived in town a few blocks away from the university.

She could still picture helping her mom, Cathy, with her garden. They never had a green thumb, so Lana helped her plant flowers, bushes, and landscape a little with lava and river rocks. She smelled roses then, opening her eyes.

Sitting on the stone bench in the corner of Cathy's backyard, Lana breathed heavy. Had she just transported? She knew she was capable of doing so but she had never tried. She never learned either.

Cathy knew of Lana's powers, so her showing up in the backyard wouldn't be a surprise.

She knocked on the back door, Rae opening it. The brunette swung the screen door open, wrapping her long arms around Lana. She pulled her inside to the living area, a small space filled with an oversized sectional and a 32-inch TV. They preferred comfort over the quality of television they watched.

"What happened? Tell me everything," Rae said, placing her hands on her legs.

Lana tried to find the words, but none came out. She stood, pacing the length of the room.

Cathy, a middle-aged woman with dirty blonde hair and reading glasses, brought a pitcher of lemonade and freshly made sugar cookies into the room, setting them down on the coffee table.

"Lana what I saw…" Rae started. "You were choking and there were flames."

Lana's hand instinctively went to the red, bruising marks on her neck where the curtain had wrapped around so quick she couldn't put her arm up to deflect the attack.

"Dimitri called it a Holanshee, an invisible banshee-like demon who attacks you using your own powers," she said softly. "You saw it?"

"Yeah, I tried to call you but your phone went straight to voicemail," Rae said. "Wiley didn't say what happened, just that I can't go home."

"Banshees are like working dogs," Cathy said. "When they have a target, they will stop at nothing until that target is eliminated. A Holanshee is similar in the fact they lie in wait until the target reappears. Once they have a set location, that is where they stay until they have completed their task."

"How do they find their target?" Lana asked.

"They didn't explain anything to you, did they?" Cathy asked softly.

"I didn't ask," Lana said.

"Typically, a Holanshee is summoned by a witch or warlock," she said. "They are given a location and they stay there until the target has appeared. They are powerful creatures, and almost impossible to kill. The only way to kill them is to find and kill the person who conjured them in the first place."

"Can a demon hunter control them?" Lana asked, her voice soft and shaky.

"Only if the demon hunter was previously a warlock," Cathy said. "In that case, vanquishing the demon and the demon hunter are a more difficult task."

Cathy left the room, descending the stairway in the hall to the basement. She returned with a weathered book like the one Roderick, her childhood friend, had many years ago. She flipped to a page with the picture of a demon hunter sketched on it. It had black hair and pitch-black eyes. The entry read:

The Demon Hunter is a man who has been called to the dark side of his magic. Born a warlock, the Demon Hunter becomes one when he travels to the Underworld during the Dark Passage. The Dark Passage is a ceremony held in the

Underworld meant to draw warlocks in to turn them into hunters. The ceremony promises a warlock the ability to see into the demon realm, and to do so, the warlock must drink demon blood while in the Underworld. The corpse of the warlock remains in the Underworld while an apparition of the man takes form in his place.

The only way to vanquish a Demon Hunter is to find his corpse in the Underworld and burn the bones.

WARNING: Destroying a Demon Hunter releases any summoned demons from his hold, but also returns any demons he has killed to their original state.

"So, if I want to get rid of the Holanshee, I must burn his bones," Lana said. "But if I do, any demons he has killed return in full force..."

"Correct," Cathy said. "Hence why I said it is a much more difficult task than one would think."

"And if I don't?" she asked.

"If you don't, the Holanshee will remain at your home," Rae's mother stated. "It will not harm those who enter the home, so Rae is safe."

"How would I even find his corpse?" Lana asked.

"I can help with that," Cathy left the room once more, descending the stairs. She rifled through a box of old maps, crystals and vials of years-old potions, returning with a vial of black liquid, a crystal and a map.

"Typically, a witch can search these maps with a crystal to find the one they are searching for," Cathy explained. "However, since I do not know the person, it is your job to search for him. To find his bones in the Underworld, you will dip the crystal into the vial, and hold the crystal above the map."

Lana placed the map on the chaise lounge of the sectional and dipped the crystal in the vial. The mixture burned her nostrils. She held up her hand, letting the crystal dangle over the map.

"Now, I want you to picture this individual in his initial state. This will be either the day you met or one of your strongest memories of him," Cathy said. The moment she closed her eyes, she saw Kyle sitting in the gazebo of the Jacobs' property clenching the old photograph of her and Micah. The crystal began to circle the map, taking her hand with it as it pinpointed Kyle's corpse.

Within seconds it stopped, pulling itself to the map like a magnet. Lana knew the forest better than most Clover Bay residents and had often gone to the exact location the crystal now rested on.

The church.

"The entrance to the Underworld in Clover Bay is beneath the old church," Lana said. "Of course, that's where it would be."

"Are you going to take Elijah?" Rae asked.

Lana thought for a moment to their conversation. When the vampires were caught, they were taken into the old church and burned. If they knew where the entrance to the Underworld was, they could have easily slipped away, and they would never have been killed in that fire. On the other hand, maybe they didn't know about the entrance and they truly died in that church. Either way, taking Elijah could cause him to question their potential existence as she was just now.

"If I take him, he may become conflicted and would not be able to help me find Kyle's body," Lana said. "Or what's left of his body, technically."

"At the same time, Elijah should know where you're going just in case something happens."

"That's a great idea, Rae. You tell him." Lana closed her eyes and thought back to the day Micah led her through the tall grass to go to church during the summer she'd spent in the Bay. The white church came into view, Lana feeling the wind on her cheeks. She'd done it again, transported herself to the old church grounds.

All that was left of the old building was a decrepit fireplace that once stood two stories high. She had never been in the basement of the building, but remembered there was a storm cellar behind the church. Hidden beneath pine needles, leaves and overgrowth, Lana found the door to the cellar, running her hands over the splintered wood for the handle.

Beneath the old church grounds, the cellar had barrels of rotted potatoes, flour, and oats, jars of questionable fluids and planks of wood for repairs when the building was in its prime.

"Are you crazy?" Elijah's voice made Lana jump. "You seriously think that going into the Underworld in your condition is a good idea… You're out of your mind."

"It's the only way to get rid of the demon, and Kyle," Lana said. "I knew if I brought you here you'd have issues and you wouldn't be able to help."

"Well I'm fine, and you're still crazy," Elijah said. "You also don't have fire to burn his bones if you find them."

"When I find them."

"Whatever."

"You know how to make a fire. Go make a torch or something."

Elijah brought a torch back after creating a small flame from a thin stick and some brush. With the cellar illuminated, the two searched the walls for a hidden passage. Behind one of the makeshift storage cabinets, Elijah saw what looked like a small knob protruding from the wall. He pushed the cabinet to the side, tugging on the knob.

A door the size of a two-foot by four-foot crawlspace crumbled, revealing a dirt hole big enough for them to crawl through. Elijah went first, leading the way with the light.

Five minutes into the crawlspace, Elijah and Lana fell through a hollow point in the path, landing in a shallow pool of water. All around them, darkness ensued, the cool smell of damp earth and sewage nauseating them. Elijah pulled Lana up the ramp and through a small archway, light not far from them. Shadows of flames danced on the walls, the torches lining the corridor.

"So where is this guy's body anyway?" Elijah whispered.

"It said under the church," Lana said. They followed the corridor until it turned, searching for a way that circled back to beneath the church.

"You there!" a dark-hooded man yelled behind them. "State your business."

Elijah motioned for Lana to get behind him, placing himself between her and the figure. "We're here to speak with Kyle."

"Why?" the man asked. Lana could see a scar across his mouth that angled up from the left side of his chin toward his right cheekbone.

"He summoned a Holanshee," Elijah stated.

The man took a step back, grabbing at one of the torches behind him. "The summoning of a Holanshee is strictly forbidden."

Elijah said nothing, strengthening his grip on Lana's wrist behind him. "Will you take me to him?"

The figure nodded, pushing past them. He took them down another corridor, this one unlit, down two flights of stone stairs and through a thick wooden door. He pushed the door to the side, lighting two additional torches inside the tomb. Lining the walls of the room were skeletons clothed in whatever they died in. Lana searched the clothed bones until she found one she recognized. Kyle wore khakis almost every day they were together. There was only one skeleton clothed in khakis.

The hooded figure walked straight to the bones, taking a vial of red liquid from his pocket.

"Kyle Thomas, Demon Hunter of Clover Bay, you are hereby relieved of duty for failing to obey a direct order and for the forbidden summoning of a greater demon, the Holanshee," the figure stated. He dropped the vial on the bones and handed the torch to Lana.

"Kyle has told me about you, Lana McDowall of Clover Bay," the figure stated. "I give you the honor of vanquishing the demon and its hunter for he has broken far too many rules."

"Thank you," Lana said softly.

"I expect you will leave as quietly as you came," the figure said. "Do not leave this room and venture further into the Underworld."

She nodded, the figure leaving and closing the door behind him. Lana dropped the torch onto Kyle's now drenched bones, the combination of flame to liquid forcing her into Elijah. The blast blew out the remaining torches, leaving them encased in darkness. Lana took Elijah's hand as the flames fizzled out, and thought of Rae's living room. The two returned to the sectional, Cathy and Rae eagerly awaiting their return.

Chapter 14

"So, he just, like, led you to him and let you burn his corpse?" Rae asked of the hooded figure in the Underworld. "Why does that seem like it was a trap?"

"He knew my name, and knew Kyle's. He said that Kyle talked about me, and that he had broken many rules, and that summoning the demon was the last straw," Lana said.

"And forbidden," Cathy stated, sipping lemonade.

"Is it forbidden because you can't kill the demon without going into the Underworld?" Rae asked.

Her mother nodded, gathering her supplies and returning them to their hiding place in the basement.

"So, what now?" Rae asked. "We go home?"

"We go home," Lana nodded.

~

A cabinet at the far side of the art room held a sketchpad with the front covered in colored sketches of mountains, a castle on fire and light beaming from clouds over the fancy architecture. A phoenix rose from ashes at the base of the castle. A lake with a moon's reflection was close to the bottom of the sketchpad.

He pulled a drawing pencil from his book bag and searched for a blank page. When he found one, he immediately began drawing Lana's face. He started on the oval shape of her face and the slight curve of her chin. He moved to her eyes then, tracing the circular shape of her pupils and shading them in lightly.

Aiden reached into his bag and pulled out a group of colored pencils, searching for a light blue and a red colored one to add a little violet to her eyes.

Perfectly imperfect.

He spent the next half hour sketching her nose and mouth, adding her hair last.

He pictured her with longer hair, but stuck with how he saw her Monday. Aiden started with her bangs, how they swept across her forehead from the left to the right and were tucked behind her ear. He pictured the Gemini zodiac tattoo behind her ear and drew it on the side of the page. He finished the drawing by adding the small diamond nose stud on her right nostril, and shading her eyelids a light lavender color.

Although he knew the sketch would never compare to how she looked in person, Aiden felt accomplished, closing the sketchpad. He hesitated, staring at the drawing on the front of the pad. The way the castle and the flames spiraled into the air and met the dark clouds mesmerized him for a moment, threatening to take him back to a place he wished to forget.

He quickly flipped the sketchpad over and left the table, heat rising to the surface and staining his cheeks and ears a bright red. He stood, taking the pad back to the cabinet where it stayed most of the time. He closed the cabinet door, walking away as quickly as he could.

Students filtered in through both entrances of the room, Aiden pushing past them until he was out of the room. At the top of the steps, he saw Rae heading to her class, free of Lana. He jogged to catch up with her, tapping her shoulder.

"Hey, you're Lana's friend, right?" he asked. "I'm Aiden."

"I'm gonna be late; sorry, I can't chat right now," Rae scurried off, leaving Aiden behind.

"What's with girls around you?" Dimitri asked.

"Why can't you leave me alone?" Aiden asked.

"Because we need you to come to the club house," Dimitri said. "It's getting harder and harder to wait for the Darkness to come to us; we need to go to them."

"We know when they're going to attack, why can't we just wait?" he asked.

Over Dimitri's shoulder, Aiden saw Lana walking toward the Art building. "Lana!"

He passed Dimitri, meeting her halfway. "I didn't see you yesterday, is everything okay?"

"Yeah, I just wasn't feeling very good," she lied. He could see plum-colored skin peeking out behind her hair she'd intentionally curled and left down. Aiden lifted it away from her neck, seeing a partially covered up bruise and a similar mark on the other side. Lana backed away, running her fingers through her hair to cover the bruises back up.

"What happened? Did that guy come back?" Aiden asked.

"Drop it, please?" she asked. She went the opposite way of the Art building, heading toward the quad.

"Lana," Aiden touched her arm. She turned to face him. "If he's hurting you…"

She blinked away tears, wet drops streamed one by one down her cheeks. Lana shrugged her shoulders, wiping tears away. "There's nothing you can do. He's gone."

"Is there anywhere you can go that's safe?" he asked.

"I said he's gone," she stared at him for a moment, watching his left eye twitch.

"Okay," he dropped the subject.

"Why aren't you in class?" she asked.

"I have a lot on my mind," he said. "As do you…"

Her eyes looked over her dirty sneakers. She'd tossed on some jeans and a baggy sweatshirt earlier, not caring what people thought of her appearance. It didn't faze Aiden, he still found her beautiful.

"I think you should go home, get some rest."

"Do you now?" she huffed.

"Hey, I'm concerned about you," Aiden said. "All I'm trying to do is make sure you're okay, and that you're safe."

"I appreciate the thought, really I do. But you can't honestly think that after everything that's happened, I'd still be…"

"I don't care if you're interested in me," Aiden said. "In fact, I've come to the realization that you aren't, and I'm okay with that."

"Then why keep trying?"

"It has nothing to do with my interest in you, and everything to do with the fact that I'm a caring individual who wants to make sure that those around me are okay…"

Dimitri chuckled. He'd never seen Aiden care about anyone other than Leressi, the sole reason the Crusade occurred. Aiden had sworn off romance after she'd betrayed him, yet here he was fawning over a woman he believed to be human.

"Thank you for your concern," she said. "I know it's not till Saturday, but will you be at the lake?"

He nodded, "I'm performing at the bonfire, yeah."

"If I don't see you before Saturday, I'll see you there." She turned on her heel and left, stuffing her books in her bag before reaching her car. Although she didn't want to return to the house, she had no other place to go than the Jacobs' manor, and even then, she didn't feel comfortable there either.

"You really like her," Dimitri stated. "What happens when she grows old and you fail to age?"

"You heard her, she's not interested," Aiden said. "I have nothing to worry about."

"If she were though," Dimitri proposed. "What if this all blows over, we destroy the Darkness, and she comes around? What would happen?"

"Her best friend is a vampire. I bet he'd turn her if she'd stay around long enough for us to tell her what we are."

"Elijah would never do that," Dimitri said. "He would never forgive himself if he did."

"Then she'd grow old and die."

"And you'd be okay with that?"

"D," he looked at the Earth Fury. "I don't understand why you're being this way."

"Now you know how I feel about your infatuation with her."

"What are you talking about?"

"It's been 400-something years and suddenly you've got a crush," Dimitri said. "Do you even know who she is? Why would a vampire be around a human and not turn or kill her?"

"What are you saying?"

"I'm just saying you should be careful. The last time this happened…"

"I know what happened last time, but it's different this time," Aiden said.

"You're sure about that?"

"Have you ever been drawn to someone so strongly you forget what you are?" His friend shook his head. "When I'm around her, I forget that I'm this…monster. I forget that at any moment someone could piss me off and I could blow up because of this uncontrollable anger within me. Something about her calms me."

Part of Dimitri wanted to tell Aiden the truth, but knew he'd disappear like he did during the Crusade. "Have you considered telling her?"

"What I am?"

"No, just how she affects you?"

"She'd think I'm crazy," Aiden shrugged.

"I think you'd be surprised," Dimitri said. "Stay alert. Christine's in a rough place and I don't think she's going to be any help this weekend."

Chapter 15

Rae hopped on Lana's bed, bouncing up and down to wake her.

"So, you know how the bonfire is tonight? Well, we're going…"

"We already said we were…" Lana said sleepily.

"According to Alexa, the theme is masquerade. There will be carnival booths all around and a huge stage in the middle, where local bands get to perform and entertain."

Any time Rae got the chance to talk, she took control, making Lana listen and comment when asked.

"We should go shopping so we can find a costume for you," Rae said. "I've only one mask so we need to find one for you before tonight."

"Does everyone have to wear a mask? Why can't I just wear a hood all night?" Lana asked.

"Because you are my friend and as my friend you will wear a mask. It's only fair," Rae said.

The costume store sat across from The Hideout, with walls adorned with puffy dresses, skimpy nurse and vampire dresses, makeup, and accessories. The girls rummaged through clearance bins, trying to find the right mask for Lana.

"I don't understand why someone would want to wear masks, you don't know who anyone is," Lana said.

"That's the point."

"No, it's not, you're signing people's death sentence. It's dangerous."

"How is it dangerous? Only certain people know about the party, and everyone knows everyone," Rae defended.

"Rachel, you know I'm right," Lana said, her tone of voice changing. "You do not understand."

"No, you don't understand Lana, and don't ever call me Rachel, you know better! Masquerades are meant to be mysterious; people have been hosting them forever. Now stop being a Debbie downer and start being normal." Rae fumed. She tossed a mask at Lana, leaving the store.

"Rae, I didn't…"

"Don't worry about it. I'm stressed about this party," Rae interrupted.

"What have I told you this whole time?" Lana took her hand, squeezing it.

"Not to worry," Rae said. "How am I supposed to do that if I know you might die tonight?"

"Because the key word is might…" Lana said. "Either way, tonight is going to be a night to remember."

May 28, 1840

"What is the occasion?" Lana asked.

"Does there need to be an occasion?" Micah returned.

His eyes met hers while bubbles rose in her stomach. Her heartbeat escalated slowly as he stepped closer.

One step, two steps.

"What would your father say if he knew you were in here?" Lana said, turning away from him. Each time he got too close, she moved away.

"Why do you do this? Haven't I shown you that you can trust me?" Micah said, unmoving.

"It is not about trust, Micah," she said softly. She knew she was hurting him, pushing him away.

"Are you incapable of caring for another?"

At that she turned. Lana had been fidgeting with the lace around her waist, picking at the hem of the velvet ribbon.

"I can't remember how to," she admitted finally, fearfully.

"I can show you how, if you let me," Micah said.

Thud.

The sole of his right shoe skid across the floor, his heels clicking together. She felt her heart skip a beat when he brushed his thumb across her cheek. Her skin was soft beneath the calluses of working in the barn. She felt her cheeks flush with heat while he trailed his fingers down her neck.

"Breathe, Lana," Micah said. She let her breath out slowly as his other hand rested on her side. He gripped the material of her skirt, pulling her close to him.

Their lips touched, a subtle motion. Lana leaned forward, their lips pressing firmly together. Micah's hand tangled in her hair, though gently. He pulled away slowly, running his fingers through the loose curls that fell down her back.

Lana caught herself before she fell into his arms, pressing her hands against his chest. Her eyes on his, a light gray, were curious. She wanted to feel his hands on her face again, in her hair, his lips on hers. She longed to be held by him, to fall asleep in his arms. It had been years since she felt another pair of lips on hers.

"Natalie will be in in a moment to help you get ready," Micah said softly. *"I'll be at the stairs to escort you to the festivities once she informs me you are ready."*

"You never told me of the occasion," Lana inquired.

"It is going to be a night to remember, Miss McDowall,"
Micah said, kissing her cheek softly.

~

The mask was a light shade of blue with intricate swirls of
white and gold, starting at the edges of the eyes and working
their way up the black feathers on either side. Silver crystals
were placed strategically on six points, acting as mirrors, and
were outlined with gold faery-like wings.

Lana placed the mask on Rae's bed, stripping to nothing
before heading into the bathroom.

"So, what are you wearing to the party?" Rae called from
the connecting closet.

"I was thinking of jeans and a hoodie," Lana answered.

"Nu-uh! You are wearing something cute, you have to!"

"Why do you insist on controlling me tonight? I want to
wear comfy clothes, let me do that ok?" she said. "Besides,
you already saw what I was wearing, so you can't argue."

Rae was silent as the water ran, fogging up the windows
of the shower. Lana let the water run over her body, through
her hair.

The water bowed then, strands of water making its way
toward the shower door. The water danced to music hummed.
As she held her hand up, the water snaked around and through
her fingers, creating the shape of a large water drop on the back
of her hand.

Drops then moved further up her arm, creating the image
of a rose, stem, and thorns. Lana smiled as the water returned
to its natural flow, rolling over her as before.

Lana turned the water off, drying off quickly. When she
returned to Rae's room, her friend scolded her.

"Are you done playing with the water? Your jeans and a hoodie are on the bed."

Rae pranced into the bathroom, slamming the door behind her.

May 28, 1840

"My, Miss McDowall, you look stunning," Micah said. He took her hand, twirling her.

"Are you going to tell me the occasion now, Mr. Jacobs?" Lana asked. Micah couldn't help but smile at the beauty before him.

He chose a lilac silk number with purple lace and underskirt. She wore black satin gloves that reached her elbows.

"What are you staring at?" she asked.

"Not staring, admiring," Micah clarified.

He placed her hand in the crook of his elbow, noticing her smile from the corner of his eye as they descended the stairs.

"Happy birthday, Lana," Micah said.

Lana squeezed his arm in thanks, blinking back tears. The last time someone acknowledged her birthday, she was holding her mother's hand as she lay dying. She told Elijah the day she got off bed rest, unaware he would remember, let alone that she'd still be in Clover Bay.

The brothers convinced her to stay; Micah convinced her to stay. When they rounded the corner, patrons in the ballroom acknowledged her, saying happy birthday and kissing her cheek or shaking her hand. Elijah and Abigale stood by the table of champagne, Elijah kissing the back of her hand, Abigale hugging her. Abigale had her moments.

Lana turned toward Micah, thanking him for the ball. "What a marvelous occasion."

"Only the best for you," Micah said.

August 23, 2018

They could feel the music in the parking lot as they pulled up to the party. Girls in stilettos and mini dresses with extravagant masks walked with men dressed in slacks and vests, ties and masks in hand.

Limousines, farm trucks, and fancy cars parked alongside Rae and Lana.

"Try to have fun tonight, okay?" Rae asked.

Lana ignored her friend, putting the mask over her face. She exited the vehicle, heading toward the party.

The music got louder as Lana and Rae approached the carnival. Booths full of stuffed animals, games, and prizes wrapped from one side of the stage, around the back to the other side. A stage showered in navy and indigo lights was in the center surrounded by a hundred masked teenagers. Lana watched Rae meet up with other people walking onto the dance floor and disappear into the mass of swaying bodies.

The bonfire was close to the lake to the right of the carnival and Lana could see Aiden and Elijah talking.

"Looks like you two are becoming best friends," Lana said, lifting her mask till it sat on her head.

"Hey," Aiden said. "Glad you could make it."

"I'm gonna go get a drink, you two want anything?" Elijah asked.

"Beer."

"Punch."

"Got it," the vampire left the two alone to enjoy the fire, the slosh of the lake dulling the music.

"Are you feeling better?" Aiden asked, taking a seat on the bench.

"Much, thank you," she said. "I'm sorry about the other day. My life is hectic right now, between Professor Thomas and school. Rae's been moody too, and I don't really know why. It's just difficult to think about adding another thing to my life."

"I get that," Aiden said. His hands were clasped in front of him, twiddling his thumbs. "Things with Christine aren't really working out."

"I'm sorry to hear that," she said.

"No, it's okay. Things haven't been good for a while, not that I don't like her, because I do. It's just…she can be a bit intense and controlling. Her life before she came here was crazy and so she… She wants more than I can provide, so to say."

"So, you don't want a relationship?" Lana asked.

"Not with Christine…" Aiden said, flames dancing in his eyes. "I don't do clingy, and that's all she is. Self-centered. Needy. I prefer someone who is independent and confident in their own skin."

"Don't we all," Lana sighed.

"I think that's why I've been trying so hard to get your attention," Aiden said, their eyes meeting. "I've had a lot of bad happen in the past and it's hard to trust people. When I'm around you, it's like all the bad goes away."

Butterflies flew in her stomach, her breath catching in her throat.

"Yo, Aiden! It's almost time for you to go up!" a slender man called from the crowd.

Aiden took a deep breath and let it out quickly, a smile on his lips. "That was a lot harder to say than I thought it would be."

A nervous laugh escaped them both. "Well, looks like that's your cue."

"I'm glad you came tonight," Aiden said. He left as Elijah walked up with drinks, grabbing the beer and jogging up to the stage.

"Thank you! You have been an awesome audience, now it's time to introduce you to a good friend of mine," the artist on the stage said as he gasped for air. "Put your hands together for AM!"

A cloaked figure stalked onto the stage, girls screaming in adoration.

"Who's ready for a party?!" AM yelled.

AM dropped his cloak, revealing chiseled abs and a red mask.

Yellow and orange flames flew from the mask, making the women scream in fear of him being burned. The flames died down, revealing glittered flames painted from the chin to the eyes, around and up to the top of the mask. Aiden turned to a guitarist who threw him a t-shirt as they began to play various solos while he pumped up the crowd. When he started singing, Lana was mesmerized by the depth of his voice.

Years of listening to the slow melodies of soul music, the saxophone during the jazz ages, of hair bands and scream, high ranges like that of the Bee Gees, made her appreciate opera-esque voices, choral melodies and orchestra music.

"What do you think of what he said?" Elijah asked.

"You were eavesdropping?" she exclaimed, the back of her hand meeting his chest. "I can't take you anywhere."

"Hey, can you blame me?" Elijah asked.

"No. I don't know, honestly. I just can't focus on romance right now, you know? It's just a distraction and at the end of the day, he's human and I can't see a life with someone who can't not age with me."

They made their way to the first set of carnival booths, debating which game to play first. She decided on a ring toss, making five of the six she threw. When told she won a stuffed animal, she declined the prize, playing for the fun of the game rather than material items.

Lana always enjoyed a good game, regardless of the reward. She'd rather play to enjoy the event, to enjoy the company of fellow players than to play for recognition and the title of winner. Material items never appealed to her, her mother taught her that.

"I get that, but still. Once you fulfill the prophecy, who's to say you won't be able to have a normal life?" Elijah asked. "I mean, I could turn him for you."

"Just like you let Micah turn?" she turned to him.

"That's a different story, Lana, and you know it."

"How is it different? If you were going to be what you are, you were going to take him with you, you said it yourself."

"Whatever," Elijah said. "I'm just saying that…'

"I know what you're saying, and it's not going to happen."

Elijah walked off, leaving Lana to play games.

As she continued to try each booth, the booths closer to the stage seemed vacant, unlike they had been earlier in the evening. She lifted her hood and putting back down her mask.

Lana took a softball at the next booth, throwing it toward the metal milk bottles. She remembered placing those empty bottles outside when milk bottle collection day occurred in her town, when they moved from metal to glass and when she no longer had milk delivered to her home. She threw ball after ball, three in a row. The clanking of the bottles falling brought back memories of when she attempted to create a small breeze and conjured a gust of wind, which sent empty bottles crashing to the hard floor of her kitchen.

She declined the prize again, tipping the game maker. Lana's name was called by a woman's voice, like Rae's, but raspier. The image of the wrinkled old witch from *Snow White* entered her mind. The music started to fade as she moved farther into the more vacant booths. Curiosity took hold, as if she was being controlled by someone or something.

"Lana," Rae's voice popped into her head. Confused, Lana thought back, *"Rae, what's going on?"*

"Lana, help me..." her voice again.

Panicked, Lana looked around. She had moved too far into vacancy where no voices or music existed. A single light in a booth ahead of her shone, a figure or shadow of a figure appeared.

"Rae..."

"Lana, help me. You need to find me." The voice sounded like Rae's but was different. It *taunted* her.

"Why don't you come find me?" Lana taunted back. The figure disappeared and Lana followed. She knew Rae was not in danger, knew the voice was not hers.

As Lana approached the booth, the light turned off, engulfing the vacant booth in darkness. Ripping her mask off, Lana threw it to the side, slipping in-between the booths and out into the forest beyond.

Chapter 16

Lana zipped her jacket up, scanning the mass of trees. Each step she took brought her farther and farther from the semicircle of tents. The hair on the back of her neck rose slightly, falling as quickly as it rose. Facing the tents, Lana's eyes darted from side to side, her ears picking up various sounds. The music from the party was nonexistent. She heard no laughter, no talking.

Silence.

Crunch.

A shadow appeared to her left, she swung, clawing at the shadow. It scattered with a screeching sound, as if her nails dug into the sheath of ectoplasm and ripped it apart. She took a few steps more into the forest. Another shadow, another sheath ripped apart, another screeching noise bounced off tree trunks, deafening her.

The further she got from the carnival, the colder the air became.

"Lana."

A raspy voice swirled in her head as she spun around, swinging from side to side, ripping through the shadows.

Laughter mocked her, taunted her as she stomped through the forest.

"Coward."

Lana crouched, listening to the sounds around her.

The caw of a crow.

The hoot of an owl.

The crunch of twigs beneath boots.

"Got ya."

Lana grasped soil, twirling around to meet the figure behind her. The broad shoulders of a man with a leather jacket that reached the backs of his knees, black pants tucked into black boots, a dark t-shirt beneath the buttons of the jacket. Gloves with revealed fingers, chin-strap beard with a mustache, salt and peppered in color, his hair black as tar and scraggily.

As she opened her hands, the man ducked, disappearing in a black cloud. She turned to run, leaning back, sliding on her knees as the man facing her now swung. Lana turned again, landing in a push-up position. Pushing herself off the ground, she sprinted back toward him, ducking and swinging her body around, leg extended to trip him, put him on his back.

Twigs and branches broke beneath the weight of him, sending sounds like bones shattering through the trees. Lana hopped over him, ran, and sprinted, swerving in between trees, sliding beneath the branches of the pines.

A large hand wrapped around her neck, picking her off the ground and slamming her to the floor of the woods. The ground shook beneath them while she pushed at his body, his hands to release her.

Lana heard screaming then.

"The party has just begun," the man's raspy voice was in her ear.

She closed her eyes, focusing on her breathing, on the elements around her. She felt rough roots wrap around her wrists, her fingers. Lana opened her eyes, pushing her hands toward the figure once more. The roots seemed to jump from her arms, wrapping around the figure's arms as he forced himself toward her. The roots tangled around him while she stumbled to her feet and ran in the direction of the row of tents, ripping through shadows threatening to keep her from her friends.

Lana took a second to look back to where she left the man tangled in roots, only to be knocked down. She scrambled to her feet, turning to run the opposite way.

~

"Rae have you seen Lana?" Elijah asked, grabbing at Rae's arm. He pulled her from her friends and into an empty booth.

"She was playing games last I saw," Rae said. "Why, what's going on?"

"I went back and she wasn't there," Elijah said. "I need you to go to your vehicle, and lock…"

Screams ran through the carnival, interrupting Elijah's train of thought.

"Eli what's happening?" Rae said.

"How well can you control your powers?"

"I don't know… I haven't practiced," she admitted.

"I need you to try, do you understand? I need you to stay behind me and if you get stuck, call my name. Do you understand?" Elijah asked.

Rae nodded, taking his hand. He broke a table apart, handing her a stake and taking one for himself.

"Vampires?" Rae asked.

She followed him toward the stage, seeing people she knew fall to the ground, blood running down their necks from bite marks. Elijah grabbed at the sleeves of one of the biters, jamming a stake through his back. Ashes covered his hand while Rae followed his movements. Together they worked their way through the vampires, staking them one by one.

Rae kept her back to Elijah, taking down each vampire who came her way. He took her wrist, pulling her closer to him.

"Stay close, I'm not going to let anything happen to you," he said.

Aiden hopped off the stage, ducking under the blue plastic covering of a booth. He ripped the leg off a table, grabbed his knife, and sharpened it into a stake. When he left the tent, a vampire grabbed him by the jacket, spinning him around and pushing him into the light posts. The creature was young, possibly turned when he was no more than fifteen years old. Aiden switched positions with him, driving the stake through his heart.

Ashes covered his boots as he made his way toward the crowd. Elijah held Rae's hand while they took down vampires around the outer areas of the crowd. Aiden worked through other vampires, being careful not to step on their victims. Ashes were spread over the bodies, blood caked in the dirt.

Elijah heard his name being called as he made his way closer to the stage.

He saw Aiden next to the light posts by the stage yelling his name. They met each other, Rae letting go while the men spoke, staking a female vampire to the ground. Black streaks like charcoal stained her face.

"Have you seen Lana?" Aiden asked.

"She headed behind the stage."

They looked around the crowd, seeing humans fighting against vampires, some overpowering the recently turned children of the Darkness. Aiden watched as Christine put vampires down with her mind.

~

A wall of dark shadows formed in front of Lana, blocking her path.

You must learn to balance each element, just as you must learn to balance good and evil.

Ms. Baldwin's words emerged within her mind. She remembered the riverbed, the flowing water over the dry rocks. The leaves rustling in the wind, and the water meeting the wind, creating clouds, precipitation, thunder. Before she turned around she felt drops of water on her face, she was conjuring a storm. She focused on the clouds, on the elements of air and of water. Lana created a dark cloud above the forest, felt the thunder rumble overhead, the rain start to soak through the thick trees.

~

Drops of rain fell from the sky, followed by powerful gusts of wind.

"What's happening?" Elijah asked.

"The others are here," Aiden whispered. "I need to find Lana, are you good here?"

"Go, Rae and I have this covered," Elijah said. When he looked back to where Rae had been, she was nowhere to be found. "Rae!"

Elijah turned toward the stage but Aiden was gone.

Although he wanted to look for Rae, the urge to kill, the violent instinct he'd worked so hard to subdue overwhelmed him. He attacked the closest vampire, ripping his throat out, followed by his heart. The vampire fell to ashes in the mud as rain cascaded around him. He threw the stake at the next vampire. Each creature that went down moved him closer and closer to a breaking point.

Elijah took hold of the next vampire's arm, turning him around to stake him. He froze as thunder boomed above them. Soaking wet, Elijah lowered his arm, as did Micah.

"We meet again, brother," Micah said, embracing his lost companion.

~

The forest was dark while Aiden ran through the mud and shadows appeared and disappeared. Thunder cracked, followed by lightning, lighting up the forest. He continued to dodge shadows, running through the forest. A thick black fog engulfed him, lifting him off the ground.

He kicked, struggled to break free. Flying through the air, Aiden collided with a tree trunk, fell to the ground, and gasped for breath. The tip of a blade touched his chin, motioning for him to rise.

"Look at you, trying to be a hero," a deep voice said. "You don't even know what you're looking for."

Aiden pushed himself to a standing position, red sparks surrounding his hands. A flash of fire illuminated the men, sending the sword-wielder tumbling to the ground. An amber sword, the blade the color of copper, formed in Aiden's left hand.

"Pick up your sword," Aiden said, challenging the man.

"Aiden, the great Ruby Fury. I am Alric," he said.

"Didn't I kill you already?" Aiden asked. He swung, the Fury's sword meeting Alric's charcoal blade, the chainmail hilt clinking. The sounds of metal clashing with metal rang in their ears.

Thunder clapped in the sky above as sheets of rain continued to drown the sound of the fight, the clash of the metal, the swings, the swooping movements, and the grace of veteran warriors. The hilt of Aiden's sword met Alric's as he spun around. He knelt, kicking at Alric's kneecap, disabling him.

The steel sword sunk in the mud created by the storm. Aiden dug the toe of his boot into Alric's chest, the tip of his sword grazing the material above the Dark acolyte's heart.

"Don't worry, this will only hurt for a moment," Aiden said.

"The girl will die, you all will!" Alric yelled before the amber sword sliced through his shirt, shattering the bone beneath.

Aiden felt the pulse of Alric's heart through the sword, each thump before the Dark servant lay lifeless beneath him. The blade glowed orange like it had been sitting in a pile of burning coals, forcing Alric's skin to burn from the inside, his bones turning to ash beneath Aiden's boot.

~

A shadow bolt knocked Lana to the ground but she pushed herself back up, grabbing soil in her hands. Fists formed, which she swung in the direction the bolt came from. Thick clumps of ground and roots were sent flying, colliding with bolts of darkness from the man pursuing her. The storm raged on, turning dirt to mud, growing vines and roots around her.

Dark shadows flew toward her, only for them to be blocked by a spiral of mud surrounding her. Lightning struck the ground again and again, forcing the man back. He conjured large blobs of melted mercury-looking creatures, sending them hurtling toward the earthy barrier keeping him from his prize.

He had been tasked to find a reason for his master to return to Clover Bay, to find one thing he'd want more than anything to obtain. She was it; she was the key to unlocking the true meaning of Darkness.

The earthen shield began to crack, falling to pieces around Lana's feet. The black lava creatures engulfed her, suffocating her screams.

It took everything within her to push away from the burning beings. She tapped into the earth once more, roots and vines wrapping around her legs, arms, and body until she pushed them out, tearing the molten creatures apart, Lana falling to her knees. She was breathing heavy, the rain ceased. Clouds broke up above the trees while boots squished and trekked through the mud.

"I thought you'd never tire," Rayaz said. He knelt in front of her, two fingers beneath her chin. Their eyes met, his pitch black, hers teal and white. "Remarkable. Donovan will be pleased to know I've found you."

"It can't be…"

A bolt of black smoke collided with her chest, sending her into a pine tree. A black and silver staff formed in his free hand, a sharp spearhead at its tip. The spear tore through her, warm scarlet liquid rushing down the bulk of the staff.

Rayaz knelt over her, pulling the staff from her torso.

She let her mind go blank, accepting she'd die tonight.

Finally, she would be free from so many years of misery, sorrow, free from running and hiding.

Mud covered her face as he searched for another identifier – a necklace or a birthmark, something to show she was truly the Amethyst Fury. As he repositioned his body, taking her head in his hands, a crimson spark illuminated them.

He was thrust backward, knocking into the pine tree. Rayaz staggered to his feet, leaning against the tree for support. He glanced at the dark figure making its way toward him and stood straight then, lifting his chin as if to challenge the Ruby Fury.

A ball of fire hurled toward Rayaz from Aiden's hand, but he dodged the attack, rolling to the side as the tree burst into flames. He wobbled, pushing himself to his feet and dragged Lana toward him, taking Lana's head in his hands, ready to snap her neck.

Aiden lowered his arm, watching the man carefully.

"Ah, you know who you are dealing with…" Rayaz said.

A dark smoke bolted from his hand toward the Fury but was dodged. Tree roots wrapped around his feet, lifting him into the air. His hand tangled in Lana's hair as he rose, waking her.

As she grabbed hold of the man's wrist, a purple gem shone from a chain around her neck. The ring glowed for a split second as Aiden took a step forward. Rayaz looked toward the source of his confinement, hearing the crackling sound of wood being burned.

"Do you know who you are dealing with?" Aiden asked.

Rayaz grunted, releasing Lana after a shock radiated from his fingertips to his shoulder blade. She landed in Aiden's arms before the flames reached Rayaz's leg, engulfing him. She looked at the burning corpse above her before they disappeared in a red haze, the action and the pain forcing the black fog at her peripheral vision to take over, knocking her unconscious once more.

~

The rain stopped suddenly as the clouds above broke into pieces, returning the night sky to a calm navy blue. Elijah and his brother looked around, noticing the straggling vampires had disappeared.

"What's going on?" Micah asked.

Elijah found Rae on the outer edge of the bodies and ash, bite marks and blood staining her neck.

"I told her I wouldn't let anything happen to her," he said.

"You can only control so much," Christine said.

"She'll be fine, her heart is still beating," Micah said.

Aiden appeared from the parking lot carrying Lana, meeting up with the others at the edge of the carnival grounds.

"Aiden, thank God you're alright," Christine said.

Aiden placed Lana on the ground gently, draping his jacket over her limp body.

Elijah had to hold Micah back, the scent of blood wafting through the air.

"What happened?" Dimitri asked, walking toward Aiden and Lana.

"She was attacked," Aiden said. "We need to get the survivors into their vehicles, the entire University population is here. If we try to take care of this mess, innocent people could lose their lives."

Elijah and Micah nodded, as did Christine. Two more men joined the blond man and received acknowledgement from Aiden.

112

Once the survivors were returned to their vehicles, Elijah was the first to speak.

"How do we 'take care of this mess'?" he asked.

"Aiden," Dimitri said.

He nodded, walking to the edge of the grounds. The light posts holding the stage lights began to buckle, melting and falling toward the carnival booths. Plastic tarps burst into flames, producing a domino effect for each of the tents. The bodies of the deceased were the next to burn, the stage engulfed in orange and blue flame. The metal frames of the stage crumpled in on itself, melting to the base posts. Puffs of black smoke rose from the flames, dancing in the sky above the chaos.

"I'll stay behind, you better get out of here before the cops show up," Christine said.

Aiden picked Lana up carefully, disappearing in a red puff of smoke. Elijah did the same with Rae as Dimitri placed his hand on his shoulder. The three of them disappeared, surrounded by a green haze.

The other men grabbed vehicles, leaving Christine and Micah alone at the wreckage with the survivors sleeping soundly in their cars.

"What are we going to tell the police exactly?" Micah asked.

"They'll believe anything," Christine said, leaning against the wooden fence post. "We'll tell them about the fire."

Chapter 17

Cool air rustled the curtains, the drying petals of flowers in a vase. In a room of white, long dark brown strands of hair draped over the pillows were the only color. Elijah paced the room, tapping his forefinger on his chin, his arm across his chest. He could hear the faint thumping of a heartbeat, the soft sound of sheets, of material rubbing against material as she breathed.

The floorboards beneath his feet creaked with each step he took, threatening to wake the lifeless body before him. Looking at her he remembered the night he brought her to his family's home. Drenched in water from a recent storm, Elijah carried Lana into a spare bedroom, a local doctor trailing not too far behind him to assess how ill she was. Once the young adults were in dry clothing, the doctor performed a checkup, informing him she had pneumonia, and all they could do was let her rest.

Slowly, Lana recuperated, waking up a few days after being taken in by the Jacobs' family. Back then, pneumonia could kill within a matter of days, sometimes hours. When Lana woke, the doctor deemed her recovery a miracle, but that she must still rest and regain her strength. Elijah and his family, after convinced by his brother, aided in her recovery, giving her a place to stay until she could be on her way.

He remembered how she looked while she was on bed rest, how frail and weak, pale and on the verge of death. Elijah hated seeing her that way once more, knowing he could do nothing to help her without the risk of her passing and turning into one of his kind.

Her skin was cold, the color of translucent paper, her hand clammy while he held it. He could still hear her heartbeat, but it had slowed, as did her breathing. He examined an artifact he'd not noticed before on her finger, a metal ring with a gem in its center. Beautiful images of various symbols embellished the sides of the ring.

"It's quite something, isn't it?" said a voice. Elijah placed her hand gently on her stomach, overlapping her right hand.

"Isn't she supposed to be getting better?" Elijah said softly, clenching his jaw.

"Not all of us recover immediately," Dimitri said. "Her opponent fed on her weaknesses. He knew what he was doing."

"Aren't you supposed to be able to heal her? Help her? She is dying; I can hear her heartbeat fading every second I sit here doing nothing!" Elijah said.

"I think you need to go into the living area, your brother and Christine have arrived," the blond man said. His green eyes were fixed on Lana when he stepped into the light.

"I remember you," Elijah said. "You were in the woods. I followed her shortly after she ran away."

"I remember," he said. "I'm not trying to be rude, Elijah, but it's better for Lana if you go into the living area. When she first recovered, you weren't watching her every moment while she was on bed rest, were you?"

Elijah wasn't aware he had known about that.

"Elijah, I understand you are not happy right now, that you want to help her and that you are hurting, everyone is right now. We nearly lost one of our own but if you wish to help her now, then listen to me. Go into the living area and be with the others," Dimitri said.

The men stared at each other for a moment before Elijah looked back at Lana. Her lips were slowly losing their blush color, and with her hair, she looked almost like a ghost.

"How did you find her?" Elijah asked. "You put that ring on her finger. How did you know what she was?"

"I didn't. That is the beauty of the ring," Dimitri said. "We had been following her for a short time. Whenever she was attacked, the ring was activated. It took me to her."

"Using a tracking spell?" Elijah asked.

"It's difficult to explain. You see, when a Fury has been born, the ring will activate. An elder can then track the Fury using a tracking spell," Dimitri said. "If a Fury has been attacked, harmed in any way other than natural illnesses, the ring will also activate."

"So, you're an 'elder?'" Elijah asked.

"Furies can also 'track' other Furies, we just have other methods, without involving outside magic's," Dimitri answered. "Our techniques allowed me to see images of a town, identifiers that could lead me to her whereabouts. I followed them, and as I got closer, the ring lit up, like a beacon of some sort. I have never had to track one of my own before, so it was an interesting process."

"How were the others found then?"

"That story is for another night," Dimitri said. "You really should go speak with your brother, he is troubled."

Elijah wanted to know more, realizing he knew just as much about what Lana was as she knew about him; nothing. Instead of arguing with Dimitri, he left in silence, floorboard creaks echoing in the hollow room.

A white feather traced itself along Rae's cheek, tickling her upper lip and below her nose when Elijah walked in. The feather disappeared when Rae rubbed her nose. He sighed, relieved at least one of them was recovering. Rae had enough life left in her to drink his blood once they got to the 'club house' as Dimitri's friend put it.

She sat up slowly when he came to sit next to her on the couch, a black faux-suede material with white stitching to accent the dark furniture.

"I'm sorry," Elijah said. "I never should have let go of your arm."

Rae tried to speak but her voice was hoarse, her throat itchy and aching.

"He really is sorry, Rachel," a woman in white said, sitting on the back cushion of the couch. She let herself slide over the back of it, holding onto the backboard. Sitting between Rae and the cushion, she looked at the Seer with large white-gray eyes, her legs folded beneath her.

"What are you?" Elijah asked, sparking the attention of the woman.

"They're called Diviners, beautiful creatures really," a topaz-eyed man said, entering from the kitchen. "Or Genies, but we call them by their names. That is Era."

The ivory-colored woman blinked quickly in Rae's direction, smiling and giggling, a high-pitched sound that made them break eye contact.

The man then pointed toward a brown-haired woman in an olive-colored dress, her skin a warm honey color. Her eyes, just as large and alien-like as Era's, matched that same honey color, with spikes of darker brown and golden green.

"She is Terra," he said.

He sat on the arm of another black furniture piece, a woman with jet-black hair and translucent skin looking up at him, her eyes a dark shade of blue. "And this is Naida."

His tone of voice went from informational to intimate as he looked back at the woman in blue. Her blouse was a shade lighter than her eyes with metal accents at the tops of her shoulders. The neckline was low, revealing a white camisole top beneath. She wore black dress pants and stiletto heels to match the color of her blouse.

"Don't mind them, they are always lovey-dovey," the Genie Era said.

"I'm Elijah, and you already know Rae's name," he said. "What is yours?"

"Wiley Ternan. I suppose you have already met Dimitri and Aiden, although I'm unsure where the latter has disappeared. EJ will be returning shortly."

"Now you're throwing out all these terms, these names yet you aren't explaining anything. Do you realize how new all of this is to us?"

"You are not a new vampire," Terra said. "You know what Rachel and Christine are, yet you don't know about us?"

"You have to understand our histories are different, Terra. Our folklore and our myth, theories," Naida said, defending his ignorance.

"Are you going to teach us? Or keep us in the dark?" Elijah prodded.

Dimitri came in then, rubbing his temples. Terra moved quickly, Elijah almost thought he saw wings. She clung to him, lacing her fingers with his and bringing his hands to his side. Their foreheads touched, eyes closed. He heard her tell him to inhale and exhale a few times, gather his thoughts.

"Diviners were created to be the acolytes of Mages. When a Diviner betrayed their Mage, all Diviners were banned from the kingdom of Caon," Era explained. "The Diviners then traveled from village to village, trying to find someone who would accept them and their abilities. Some tried to show the villagers how to improve their way of life."

"Wait, kingdom? I've never heard of that kingdom, and I spent plenty of time with the Royal families in Europe studying their history," Elijah said.

"We're not from your world, vampire," Naida said sweetly.

Era continued her story once Elijah was silent. She said Diviners were accepted in the village of Shadowspar, rumored to be the birthplace of dark magic in Sumardana, the world they come from. The village was on the outer rim of Alduin Par, a kingdom on the brink of extinction controlled by a Mage with cruel intentions, or so Era said.

"Diviners found a home in Shadowspar," she said. "They needed someone to accept them and found that the villagers needed them as much as they needed the villagers. Diviners, known for their illusions, hunted down a water source, bringing fresh water to the fields through an irrigation system and taught the villagers how to create weapons from natural resources, how to hunt, and how to survive."

"Little did the Diviners know," Era spoke softly, "they themselves were being hunted."

"That's enough Era, story time is over," Dimitri said. "Has anyone seen Aiden?"

"If you're looking for the hot head, he's out in the yard playing with fire," Christine said as her and Micah came in from off the balcony. She grabbed his arm, taking a seat across from Elijah and Rae.

Dimitri didn't say anything, only left the room and his Diviner behind. The air grew cold, illuminated by red and orange lights coming from outside.

"He always does this; don't pay him any mind," Wiley said. "Era, shall we continue on with the story?"

Elijah broke in, "I think we've heard enough for one night. Rae needs to rest."

"But I just got here, brother, can't you stay a little longer?" Micah asked.

"No, Micah. There are more important things to handle here than to be taught a history lesson," Elijah said. He picked Rae up, turning to Naida and Wiley. "Is there a spare room Rae can use?"

Naida nodded and led Elijah out of the living area. The hallways were dark, lit only by elegant candles in candelabras on either side of the hallway. Mirrors lined the passageway, and a large portrait hung on the far wall. The painting was of a family, or rather, of the men he'd met over the last few hours. Dimitri was sitting in a high-backed chair the color of mahogany with elemental symbols etched into the wooden frame.

Aiden and Wiley sat on either side of Dimitri, the man he figured was EJ in front of the other men. Elijah wondered where the women were or if the painting had been constructed prior to their existence with the Furies.

"Dimitri is the oldest," Naida said, noticing Elijah engrossed in the painting. "Aiden and Wiley are the youngest, and EJ is in the middle. This painting was painted more than 500 years ago when they were of age to assume the full responsibility of the Fury. Every time they see this, they want to destroy it."

"Why don't they?" Elijah asked.

"Because it's all they have left of who they used to be," Naida said. "They use it as a reminder of a simpler time, use it when they have lost themselves and need a reality check."

They took a left down another corridor, lit with more candelabras, paintings lining the hallway. Each painting was of a landscape, or a map, a person, another family. The hallways reminded him of those of a castle, lined with memories of past families and the history that goes along with the kingdom. Elijah returned to reality when the click of a lock sounded in the hallowed hall.

"Your room is across the hall, and here is your key," she said. "It was nice to meet both of you. I know we've given you a lot of information to process and it will not end here, but it will all make sense in time. Have a good night, Elijah."

Naida vanished in a cloud of glitter and smoke, like a magic trick without a trap door or bright flash of light. Rae stayed motionless in his arms while he walked her to the dark bed. This room was set up much like Lana's, only the curtains in the room were black velvet, the bedding and furniture a luscious ruby color, silky like satin against skin.

He brought the covers up to her chin, listening to her heartbeat as she breathed. Elijah wished he could be human again, seeing how humans wasted their lives away, drinking and throwing themselves at danger or sitting, watching opportunities walk in and out in the blink of an eye. He saw people destroy their bodies, their lungs, their livers, saw how they treated their friends and family, used them, betrayed them. He wondered why people were so corrupt, why they had to manipulate others to get what they wanted out of life.

Sometimes Elijah wished he could end his own life so he didn't have to watch everyone else suffer from the choices they made, watch them complain and do nothing to fix what they ruined. He wished he didn't have to feel, didn't have to suffer along with them. But suffering along with them reminded him of why he became a vampire, of why he chose to continue with the transformation, continue the bloodline. It was his duty to help end the corruption, to find the disease and destroy it.

"You can't destroy what doesn't exist," Rae said softly. "Humanity and human nature, they are natural, and if you destroy them, you destroy yourself."

He blew the candle out, engulfing the room in darkness.

Chapter 18

Light teal eyes surrounded by a golden orange ring watched as tree after tree in the yard burst into flames. The flames would then disappear, leaving the trees unharmed. That was the beauty of fire, he could use it to harm, or he could use it to entertain, all without hurting anyone or anything. His arms resting against the railing, Aiden closed his eyes.

He felt heat against his face, saw light dancing through his eyelids, and the purple veins of his eyelids illuminated by the movement of fire. Pressure fell upon his shoulders then, turning him around. The pressure was there again, followed by a gentle shaking.

"Aiden cut it out!" he heard a voice say. When he opened his eyes, Dimitri was standing before him, hands on his biceps, the reflection of dancing flames in the windows behind the other Fury.

He jerked away from his friend, simmering the flames back to nothing. The trees crumpled to ash, blackening the ground.

"What the hell is wrong with you?" Dimitri asked. "You could give away our position."

"Let them find us, I mean what they want is on her deathbed in the house," Aiden said, an open palm toward the window. "I mean what do they want with her anyway? She's just a fucking human."

"Aiden stop being ridiculous," Dimitri said.

"How am I being ridiculous? Have you paid no attention?" Aiden asked.

"What are you talking about?"

"This is how it begins, Dimitri, and it's happening again, don't you see?"

"You underestimate our power," Dimitri said.

"We are not strong enough."

"Do you even know who you've become infatuated with?"

"Lana is human, Dimitri. A being with no business messing with powers she knows nothing of."

"You honestly think she intentionally conjured the Darkness? Are you insane?"

"Why else would she be with the Darkness?"

"Lana is much more than you think."

"You need to stay away from her. Once she is healed, she's going home," Aiden said.

Vines started growing, wrapping around the railing of the balcony, bending and reshaping the metal framing. "I found her. I started training her. Aiden, she is more than we have ever encountered."

Fire engulfed the vines, the metal glowing a bright orange beneath the flames. "What do you mean you started training her?"

"Lana is not human!" Dimitri said, his voice rising.

"No, you're lying." He shook his head in disbelief. "I would know if she was anything other than just that…"

The fire slowly diminished the metal crackling from the heat.

"She's human, she has to be human," Aiden mumbled.

"Why won't you open your eyes and see what is right in front of you? Why else would she calm you when she's around? Mother Nature. The Amethyst Fury. It's all right in front of you, Aiden, if you just open your eyes!"

"Lana is human, she has to be human," the Ruby Fury mumbled once more, stumbling over a wooden table behind him. He hit the concrete hard, looking back at the Emerald Fury. "I don't care what you say. Lana is human, and I'm going to prove it!"

"Aiden, wait," but he was already gone, sending sparks and flames toward the ground.

~

"You really must be quieter when you're talking about people, you could have woken her," Elijah said when Dimitri walked in. He was sitting in a white leather armchair in the corner, watching Lana's frail frame slowly regain color. "Her heart rate has increased, but only slightly. There's no telling how long until she wakes, if she wakes."

"She will wake, Elijah." Dimitri sounded tired as he spoke.

"You baited me with my brother, why?" Elijah asked.

"I needed you to leave so I could help Lana," he answered. "For that I am truly sorry."

"Can we get back to the story?"

"I told you, that story is for another night, and it is still tonight."

"I've had enough deceit for a night, Dimitri. Either you tell me straight forward what you are and what you want with Lana, or I'm taking her away and you will lose the precious 'Fury' you tried so hard to bring out of her," Elijah threatened.

"You can't 'bring' a Fury out of someone, if that were possible she wouldn't exist. None of us would."

Dimitri stroked her cheek, and a bright yellow flower formed, the stem growing from under her nightgown, wrapping around her neck and under her chin. A spiraling leaf grew from the stem and around her ear. A yellow blossom, the shape of a tear, drooped beneath her eye on her cheek.

"The White Dragontear," he said. "A symbol of life, and of strength, the flower reveals itself to only the purest of souls. Lana's soul is pure."

"Is yours?" Elijah asked.

"Mine was, many years ago. Elijah, Lana needs to stay with us. She needs to train, and she needs to recover from this on her own terms."

"You mean on your terms. I've seen this side of her before, I watched as she nearly died and came back to life, a miracle."

"It wasn't a miracle, Elijah, it was magic. It was her magic, her lifeblood. It was as it always has been for us. We heal over time, much like you do. Some…techniques hurry the process along. The revealing of the White Dragontear symbolizes that her recovery will be quick, but her strength will take time to regenerate."

"She needs this to go away. Lana doesn't want this life," Elijah said.

"She was chosen, she must…" Dimitri was cut off.

"No more of this she must do this, she will do that. Lana can make her own decisions. When she wakes, she will do just that. This conversation, your myths, and your lore are over."

Elijah left the room swiftly, barely moving a curtain. Dimitri placed his hands over his face, feeling the calluses at his cheeks, the pressure of his elbows against his thighs while he sat. Jade eyes glanced from Lana's youthful features to the

Dragontear resting on her cheekbone. Her hands still rested on her stomach in the position Elijah had placed them before, the ring the only jewelry she wore.

Purple tendrils of hair wrapped black curls resting on her shoulders. Her lips pursed, Lana looked like she was ready to be placed in a coffin, her pale skin the symbol of death, of blood refusing to pump through her veins.

"The White Dragontear will heal you, and you will wake," Dimitri said, barely able to make a sound. "You have to wake, this can't be the end. The Darkness will find us if you don't."

Her ring finger twitched, neon green markings wrapped around her arm, the flower budding from its stem every few inches until spiraling leaves wrapped around the ring. The amethyst gem lit momentarily but grew dark, the flower and its stem and leaves fading to nothing. He dropped his head in his hands, hopelessness engulfing him.

~

Lava flowed from a gash in the mountainside, charring the ground as it rolled down the slope. Trees burst into flames on contact with the lava, the ground rumbling. Solid plates of dirt waved on the floor of the forest, orange and reddish lava visible through the cracks.

Windows shook with the rumbling of the ground, causing vases and chandeliers to vibrate and fall to the floor.

"Will someone please tell the fire child to knock it off?" a blond-haired man with dimples asked, sitting next to Era after grabbing a plate from the kitchen. Christine ordered pizza, enjoying the company of the Furies and their Diviners.

"You know how he gets, EJ," Wiley said, taking a large bite of a pepperoni-covered pizza slice.

127

"I don't care, he's going to wake the others," EJ said. He propped his feet up on the white end-table, his almost spotless white Converse shoes clashing with his light gray skinny jeans. Era laid her head on his lap, looking up at him with white eyes.

"Don't look at me like that, you know better," he joked.

Another tremor shook the clubhouse again, sending a large mirror above the mantel of a fireplace to the floor, shattering the reflecting glass.

"So, your powers are controlled by your emotions?" Micah asked, his arm wrapped around Christine's shoulder.

"Think of it like a volcano," EJ said. "A calm, dormant volcano, kind of like Lana, will stay dormant and calm. Once its emotions are triggered, it becomes more and more unstable, resulting in an eruption. When it comes to Aiden well, the eruption is literal."

"How do you calm down an angry volcano?" Micah asked.

"You let it work it out," EJ said. "That's what makes Diviners such a good addition to our lives, they know how to calm us down." He kissed Era on the forehead.

"And in Aiden's case?" Micah said.

The others looked at each other, contemplating a response.

"Aiden is angry," Naida said, careful of what to say. "It is difficult to calm him down when he is acting upon pure instinct. If someone was to confront him, that person would not succeed. That person may end up dead because he won't know how much power he is using against them."

"So, we're just supposed to sit back while he destroys the entire valley? Marches into the town and burns every house down? Starts a wildfire? Unleashes a volcano?"

"Aiden will calm down, he always does," Dimitri said, coming in from the hallway after leaving Lana's room. "He comes off the high himself, and that's the way it has to be."

"What about the people who attacked? Won't they be able to find us because of his little tantrum?" Christine asked.

"If anyone attempts to confront him, he could seriously harm them," Dimitri said. "I suggest everyone get some sleep, we've had a long evening, and it's only going to get worse from here. We knew this would happen, thanks to Rae's vision, and we need to prepare for what is coming. Era please escort Micah to his room. Christine, obviously you know where to go, this is your home too. Naida, I need to steal Wiley for a moment so we can work out a strategy."

The Furies and Diviners nodded, parting ways as the Emerald Fury sent them away.

"Lana is weak, and she needs to be protected," he said. "With Aiden…"

"Erupting?" EJ joked.

"This is not a laughing matter, Erion," Dimitri said, growling at his counterpart. "We need to find him and calm him down before he puts himself, the others and more importantly, Lana, in any more danger. The Bay is no longer safe, and we must relocate if we are to prepare properly."

"What do you need us to do?" Wiley asked.

"We need to stop the fires first, the girls will be able to find another location for training," Dimitri said.

~

"The girl will die, you all will." The words ran through Aiden's mind as he gripped the cool, damp earth beneath him. Lava flowed from large holes in the wall, filling a trench along the curve of the cave. On the surface of the lava sat chunks of earth lit on fire that reached the roof of the cave.

"She's human, Lana has to be human," Aiden mumbled, his eyes the color of blood. An orange curled line was woven in the red iris. Liquid stained his cheeks sticky, black smudges of dirt caked in the tears. He hurled balls of fire outside the mouth of the cave, lighting everything in their path on fire.

"Aiden. You need to stop this nonsense." He heard a voice say.

He spun in circles, trying to decipher whose voice he was hearing. Seeing no figures, he continued to punch gashes into the soil, revealing molten liquid beneath him.

A translucent figure appeared at the mouth of the cave, walking on the charred ground, the heat not phasing it.

"Aiden, this is ridiculous." He spun again, hurtling another ball of fire in the direction of the figure. When he saw the figure, he built a wall of fire to keep her out. She was youthful, that was what attracted him to her originally.

"Go away!" he yelled. "This is your fault."

~

She was surrounded by a wall of fire, heard the crackle of burning wood around her. She tried to cough but her lungs had no reason to. No smoke existed around her, only fire and the smell of trees turned to ash. Lana looked down at her feet, noticing she wasn't wearing shoes, or the jeans she remembered wearing at the carnival. Her feet were an odd shade of blue, almost transparent and the dress she wore reached her calves.

The straps were thin and the dress clung to her body like she had been drenched in water. When she took a step, she felt nothing beneath her feet, but saw the ground below.

"Go away! This is your fault." *She heard a male voice say.*

"You need to stop this, she needs you!" her mouth moved, but her voice did not come out.

"You're lying," the male voice said. *She noticed it the second time, Aiden.*

"Aiden, listen to me, Lana needs you. I wouldn't be here if there wasn't a reason," the voice coming from the body she was in said.

Lana's eyes moved back and forth beneath her eyelids, her fingers twitching. The White Dragontear appeared again, the amethyst stone glowing faintly. Light smoke began to wrap itself around her, under her head, neck, arms, beneath the blankets until her body seemed to disappear completely, leaving the bed and room empty.

~

"You need to stop this, she needs you," he heard again.

"You're lying; all you ever do is lie!" Aiden yelled. He dropped the wall of fire, his arms engulfed in flaming vines, his hands clenched into fists.

He stared at the figure, waiting to hear another lie. She didn't speak, only looked back at him.

"Lana needs you," she said, her voice echoing. She turned her body so Aiden could see behind her. Lana appeared, surrounded by white smoke momentarily, her hands still folded neatly on her stomach. The White Dragontear shone bright on her cheek, down and around her neck, her left arm, and around her hand and fingers.

"Dragontear..." he said breathlessly. He was beside her then, the fire around them simmering down to nothing. The ground stopped rumbling and the lava disappeared almost instantaneously. His eyes returned to a dull blue, a bright red rim around the iris fading to nothing. "Why did you bring her out here? She could have been hurt."

"She brought herself out here, through me," the vision said.

Lana's chest rose and fell, her eyes no longer moving rapidly. Instead, she blinked, inhaling deeply when she opened her eyes. The White Dragontear disappeared when she saw Aiden leaning over her. An image of a man with blood-red eyes surrounded by fire flashed in her mind, causing her to look away from him.

"Lana," Aiden's voice was soft, his hand on her cheek smooth when he touched her. "Don't be afraid, everything is going to be alright."

"I saw fire, a monster. Aiden, where are we?" she asked, tears falling from her eyes. He picked her up, her arms wrapped around his neck.

He didn't speak, only walked through the forest, making no attempt to stop when he heard twigs crunching in the distance or wolves howling at the moon on the mountain. The figure appeared and disappeared when he walked past her.

"Aiden? Did you see that?" Lana asked. When the figure appeared again she asked him to stop. "Do you see her?"

"Your mind is playing tricks on you, Lana. I need to get you home so you can sleep; you've had a rough night," Aiden said, pulling her away from the figure.

"You won't tell her you can see me too," he heard in his head. Aiden shook the voice away.

"I'm not crazy," Lana said softly. "I know what I saw."

"Fine, I will." The figure morphed inside Lana's body, visions of another world passing through her mind. Lana saw a black-haired woman with bright green eyes holding hands with a brown-haired man dressed in armor. The woman wore

132

a red dress, laced down the back with black velvet and had her hair braided with ribbons interlaced within the braid.

They were beneath a cherry blossom tree in full bloom, bushels of pink and white flowers looming above their heads. The couple was in love, they danced beneath the tree before screams echoed through the valley. The soldier released her hand, drawing his sword before heading back to the castle. She took his hand, spun him around to face her.

"I'm sorry, Aiden," Lana heard the girl say. Her eyes became large spheres, fingernails turned into sharp claws and fangs dropped from her gums. She slashed her hand across his armored chest, the plate of metal falling in pieces to the ground. His chest began to bleed and she slashed his face. He fell unconscious before she left him lying on the ground beneath the tree, the petals of the flowers falling all around him like snowflakes.

Aiden laid Lana on the ground, placing his hand on her chest. Whispering into her ear, a bright blue film surrounded his hand as he pulled it away. The blue aura turned into flames when he clenched his hand into a fist and slammed it into the ground. Light gray dust spread around his hand and the voices and visions stopped. Tears stained his cheeks and his hands when he placed his face in them, sobbing.

"Aiden? Lana?" Dimitri said, leaning next to the girl in white. "Aiden what happened?"

"Essi...Leressi..." he sobbed. "Leressi."

Dimitri picked Lana up, the three of them disappearing in a rainbow of fog.

Chapter 19

Dimitri placed Lana on the bed, pulling the sheets to her chest. She opened her eyes slowly, the image of the Fury beside her blurry.

"Where am I?" she asked softly, her voice raspy.

"You're safe now," Dimitri said. He sat on the edge of the bed, Lana sliding to the side so he had more room to sit.

"I remember you, you saved me," Lana said, her memories of him foggy. "What happened?"

"Many years ago, yes, I did," he said. He twisted the ring around his finger, its emerald stone glimmering in the candlelight. "Members of the Darkness have found you, Lana. We intercepted them at the carnival grounds and put two of them down, but they will return again."

Her skin paled and her eyes drooped from the weight of exhaustion. "Where's Rae? I need to see her."

Dimitri placed the palm of his hand against her cheek, stroking the skin with his thumb. Her shoulders sunk into the pillows, her body falling heavy against the mattress. With a single stroke, she fell asleep, a deep sleep she needed.

"We move in the morning, but for now, rest, my dear *Candra*," Dimitri whispered.

~

Small luggage piled up on the couch, Dimitri and Terra speaking in low tones while Wiley and EJ grabbed what they needed from the clubhouse. Their Diviners huddled in a recliner, grabbing at each other's hair and whispering with their high-pitched frequencies the Furies could never hear.

Out on the balcony, Micah and Christine stood close, leaning against the railing that burned and overgrew the night before.

"So, you know these guys pretty well?" Micah asked, his green eyes gazing over the ash created by Aiden's temper tantrum.

"Not really," she said, looking at him. "They keep me in the dark on a lot of things."

"Then why do you stick around?" he asked, meeting her gaze.

"They need me, I'm their Seer," Christine answered. Micah's reaction to the word 'seer' made her smile.

"So, you're a fortune teller, that's handy," Micah said. Christine didn't find it amusing; instead, she greeted him with a punch to the stomach. "How accurate are your visions?" he asked, rather strained.

"Not very... I see bits and pieces of what is going to happen," she said, a tinge of sadness in her voice. "I knew something bad would happen last night, and I warned Aiden, but most of the time I don't know when something is going to happen, it just does."

Christine turned and walked toward the sliding doors, memories of the past flooding her mind. She placed her hand on the glass, a sharp pain between her eyes stopping her from opening it. It started at the top of her nose, in between her eyebrows and moved its way up her forehead and around the curve of her skull to the back of her neck. She placed her free hand at the base of her neck, digging her nails into the skin. Clenching her teeth, she screamed, Micah placing his hands on her shoulders to steady her.

The tan brunette rocked herself back and forth, her hands covering her ears. Her head was tucked into her chest as she mumbled words Micah could barely hear.

"Don't take me back, don't take me back," Christine whispered. The Diviners and Furies stood on the other side of the glass doors, staring at the Seer tucked into the fetal position.

Micah placed his hand on her shoulder, grabbing one of her wrists. He brought his face closer to her ear to whisper but was greeted with sharp nails slashing his right cheek open. Her eyes were red with tears, her cheeks sticky with the liquid.

"I'm not crazy, don't send me back there," she said, sobbing. Turning around, she stared at the others staring back at her. "I'm not crazy, don't send me back there!"

She turned and ran, jumping off the balcony. After landing on her feet, agile like a cat, Christine continued running into the woods, leaving everything behind. She didn't look back, not at Micah, Dimitri, EJ, or the house. Instead, she looked forward, through the ash Aiden created, through the gashes in the mountainside. She could never understand her power, or what she was, and knew neither could the Furies. She had given them the time they asked her for, and there was no more left. She needed answers, needed to know what she was, and why she was made.

A wave of warmth went through her, and she noticed she was not running through the forest any longer, but through a grass field. Daisies and Dandelions blew in the wind, their fragrance filling her nose. She stopped, breathing in the sweet scent. Although it brought back a sad and terrifying memory, she turned around, and stared at her childhood home.

The house was distressed, its baseboards rotted and old. The weeping willow beside the house slumped, its branches reaching the ground, brittle and broken. The paint on the wooden siding was so badly chipped, the color was unrecognizable. With the front door hanging off its hinges, the windows had been broken as if someone threw bricks through them. This wasn't the house she remembered leaving with her mother.

Christine stood at the bottom of the stairs, looking through the doorway. Inside the house was dark; she couldn't make out any furniture. Taking the first step of the stairs, the wood splintered beneath her foot. The second wooden board broke in half, trapping her ankle between the ragged wood pieces. Her hands met the porch hard. She thought she saw movement in the home, and the sound of footsteps and old boards creaking. Before she could get her foot free, the barrel of a shotgun was touching her forehead.

"Get on up, all slow-like," said a man with a southern accent. She did as he said, standing tall after getting her foot unstuck.

He kept the gun pointed at her, his green eyes looking her up and down. "Who are you?"

Christine didn't answer. The man cocked the shotgun, placing his finger on the trigger.

"Who. Are. You?" he repeated slowly.

"Your daughter," she said. "It's Christine. Don't you remember me?"

He blinked and put the gun to his side, stepping closer to her. She sighed, smiling. The man grabbed a handful of her hair, pulling her into the house. Instead of a living room, the doorway led straight to the basement where Christine could smell decay. She tried to get free but he only gripped her neck, pushing her head toward the ground.

The shotgun clanked on a metal table, bleach and alcohol burning her nose hairs. The man placed his arm behind her knees, cradling her in his arms before placing her in a chair she recognized as one she'd sat in at a dentist's office. This one had been modified though with clamps at one end for her ankles and in the middle for her wrists.

The bloodstained metal clamps had sharp studs in them that dug into her skin when the man clamped each one onto her ankles. When he started tightening the clamps, she screamed. This alarmed the man, causing him to slam her head into the headrest of the chair. A leather strap greeted her forehead, fastening close to her right ear. All that was free were her hands now, which he proceeded to secure.

She could feel wet liquid rolling down her cheeks. "Why are you doing this?"

"Yer a monster," he said. "Ye deserve ta die."

"Is this what you did to mom? Strap her to a table thinking she was a monster?" Christine asked. "How could you do that to someone you claimed to love?"

The clamp for her left wrist had rusted nails on the inside, digging into her skin through the tissue and bone when he fastened the clamp. The other clamp came last, making her scream once more. She tried to fight against him but she had no true power.

C'mon, c'mon please show me something, she thought.

A searing pain started between her eyebrows, rolling up her forehead and around her skull to the base of her neck. Christine saw a bright white light, the man with a surgical saw in hand. He was laughing maniacally, her scared reflection in his protective glasses.

The man stopped laughing, looking down at his feet. She couldn't move, and she saw a blue light fill the room.

When she came back to reality, she saw the man staring at her, a surgical saw in hand. He started laughing like in her vision and she thrashed in the bindings, trying to free herself. She knew it was no use but also knew there wasn't long before someone came for her. The bright light was over her, illuminating her upper torso.

Christine could hear running water like a river in the distance. The man stopped laughing, looking down at his feet. When he lifted his leg and put it down, she heard a splash. She started screaming, the man lifting the saw above his head.

"She's down there!" she heard. The water started filling the room, like a dam had been open, releasing gallons upon gallons of water into the tiny space. Christine held her breath, watching the man panic. The water was up to her head, then to the lamp two feet above her face. When the man started to float, a hand grabbed at his bicep, pulling him down.

She saw a black-headed man with a ragged-edged dagger in hand spin the man she once remembered as her father around to face him. He plunged the dagger through the man's heart, turning the water a bright red. The water drained out of the room then, making small puddles on the ground.

"You're safe now, Christine, I've got you," Wiley said. Micah was beside her then opposite the Fury, aiding in the removal of the studded bindings. "Never run away again, do you understand?"

She nodded, coughing when the men broke the clamps securing her to the chair. They distracted her from the pain.

Once she was free, the three retreated from the rank room in a
blue translucent haze.

Chapter 20

Wiley placed Christine on the couch, Naida kneeling beside him. She placed her left hand on Christine's forehead, and her right over her heart. Closing her eyes, her hands began to glow a dull blue hue, sinking beneath the skin. The puncture wounds on Christine's wrists and ankles began to glow as well, healing from the inside out. Light pink scars lined her skin where the wounds were moments before.

When she woke, she saw each Fury lining the wall in front of her, their Diviners next to them and the pile of luggage, unmoved from where it had been before she left.

"Why haven't you all left yet?" she asked.

"We couldn't leave you behind," Micah said.

Dimitri waved them all to gather around him. "Everyone, please take the hands of those on either side of you."

They all held hands until the group stood in a circle around the luggage. Closing his eyes, he saw a room with salmon-colored wallpaper, a border of yellow and green butterflies close to the ceiling and tall bookshelves. There was a table in the center of the room stacked with various pages and scrolls. Chairs littered the room, some standing upright and some on their side. Large bay windows had their curtains drawn, so the only light coming into the room came from the chandelier attached to the vaulted ceiling.

He then pictured them all within the room, standing next to the table. One by one they released their grips on one another, and Micah led Christine to a red velvet divan in the corner of the room next to a high bay window.

"What is this place?" Rae said.

"Follow me, and I'll show you," Terra said.

Large doors opened wide, banging against the wall. A tall man with salt and pepper hair to his shoulders stood in the doorway, two young women by his side. He wore a gray suit with a red and black paisley tie. The woman to his left was a short blonde with one brown and one green eye. Her pencil skirt came to her knees and her crimson heels made her as tall as the man's shoulders. The girl on his right was a mousy brunette with large round glasses, a notebook, and pencil clutched to her chest.

The man spoke first, his eyes locked on Dimitri. "I'm sorry. I didn't authorize your visit."

"We needed a safe place to stay, and this was the only place safe enough for us to come," Dimitri said.

"You say that like I'm going to let you and your...friends stay here, *Fury*," the man said, scrunching his nose.

"Benedict, we don't have the time to stew over the past," Dimitri said. "This world is in danger, and if we don't do something about it, innocent people will die. And the people you are trying to protect will as well."

The short blonde girl took a step forward and another until she was face to face with Dimitri. Tilting her head to the right, she looked him over. The blond of his hair was beginning to fade, the signs of aging showing at the roots. Although she was never taught in depth about the Furies, she knew the ones who existed never aged or showed signs of aging unless times of distress were upon them.

"Tell me Fury, what is coming?" He heard in his head.

Dimitri instead placed a single finger to her temple, providing her with a vision of the Darkness at the carnival. He took the memory from Lana, the battle she fought with Rayaz and the final moment when Aiden caught her before the Dark apprentice burst into flames.

She took a few steps back, turning to speak with her master.

"So, you're telling me the Darkness has made its way to this world?" he said, chuckling. "And why are you bringing this plague to my Academy?"

"This conversation is better had behind closed doors," Dimitri stated.

Benedict looked from the line of Furies and Diviners to Micah and Christine in the corner and back. He pursed his lips, knowing he couldn't argue with Dimitri.

"Girls, stay here and make sure none of them touch anything," he said finally.

Dimitri turned to EJ, leaning close to speak with him. "Head back to the house, bring Lana and Elijah with you."

"What about Aiden?" he asked.

Dimitri closed his eyes, knowing he was only keeping Benedict waiting and impatient. "I'm more worried about getting Lana here than I am about Aiden. If he has his head on straight, he'll find us. Hurry, Benedict will need convincing and she's our only hope right now."

EJ and Era left for the clubhouse while Dimitri followed Benedict out of the large study. The doors closed behind them, leaving his apprentices with their guests.

"Past aside, I didn't know where else to turn, Benedict," Dimitri said.

"You can't expect me to say yes, regardless of what you throw in front of me," Benedict responded. "This place is a sanctuary, a temple for people like us who are not accepted in the human world. And you're insulting what I've built by even being here."

He turned to face Dimitri, stopping in the middle of the hallway. "I'm sorry Benedict but we need this sanctuary as much as you do if not more."

"And why is that?" Benedict asked.

"Do you remember when we first met? Somehow, we managed to find this place after everything crumbled and fell apart. Do you remember what we told you?"

"Yes, but what makes you think I am anything like I was back then?" Benedict said.

"Your mission is to protect the magical from the mundane. It always has been, and you protected us when we had nothing, when we knew nothing of this new world you brought us to," Dimitri explained. "The Darkness will stop at nothing to get what we have and the only way to protect that is to bring her here. All we need is a few days."

"Who are you trying to protect? The girl in the corner?" Benedict asked.

"Someone far more powerful than we ever imagined," Dimitri said in hushed tones. "We found the Light."

Benedict's eyes went wide, unsure if he heard the Fury correctly.

"She's in danger, the Darkness has found her and she is not fully trained. She really doesn't even know what she truly is," Dimitri continued. "If you could let us stay so we can finish training her, it would be very helpful. We can ensure no harm will come to this school, Benedict. But we have nowhere else to go."

"I see... I'll have Clara and Sala prepare your rooms," Benedict said slowly. "Is there anyone who needs medical care?"

"Christine possibly, she's a..."

"Seer, I know. What about the other girl?" Benedict asked.

"Rachel, yes her as well," Dimitri said. "She too is a Seer."

"Is there anything else you need from me? The Seers, how well do they know what they are?"

"I know you're going out of your way to allow us to stay," Dimitri said. "I really can't ask you to do much more."

"I don't want unstable ignorant creatures in my Academy," Benedict said. "They will receive training here, and you will not argue with me any longer."

Dimitri stayed silent, unable to speak. This wasn't the first time Benedict used this trick on him. In retrospect, their feud was more childish than anything.

Benedict had a sly grin, turning toward the study. When the doors opened, his acolytes flocked to his side.

"Ladies, please show our guests to their rooms. Christine and Rachel need medical attention so please show them to the infirmary first thing. Dimitri, if you need anything else, please don't hesitate to ask," Benedict said, leaving the women behind to follow his orders.

The blonde girl rounded up Micah, Christine, and Rachel, introducing herself as Clara before leading them down a plethora of complicated hallways until they reached their destination. Clara told Micah to stay outside when she took both girls' hands and brought them through the door. It seemed more like water when they appeared on the other side drenched.

"Don't worry, it happens to everyone," Clara said. "Come, the doctor will see you now."

Christine was motioned to sit on a small plastic table while the doctor pulled a curtain around a circular rod until the two were separated from Rae and Clara.

"Now, tell me what your ailments are," the man with a fuzzy white beard said. He had baby blue eyes surrounded by wrinkled skin.

"My wrists and ankles," she said. She held out her hands, the pink scars from where the nails clamped together bright under the light from the skylight window.

She heard the doctor hum, taking her wrists in his hands. The skin was cool and rough with age, but gentle and steady with experience. Christine felt a surge of warmth and a light shock to her wrists. When he removed his hands, the pink scars faded to a light red, the pain no longer there. He repeated the process on her ankles, asking her to lie down and close her eyes.

The shock was slightly more powerful but when he pulled his hands away, she only felt warmth.

"You should start feeling better in a few hours, my dear," the old man said. "Now send your friend in."

Christine didn't hesitate to leave the curtained room and send Rae in, but before she opened the curtain, Christine grabbed her arm.

"You'll feel a shock, but it'll be okay," she warned.

Rae managed a smile, unsure why Christine was being so kind to her.

When she saw the old man, she feared him.

"What's the matter, dear? I won't hurt you," he said. "Please, have a seat and tell me your ailments."

"I feel like I know you," Rae said, taking a seat. "But I don't know from where."

The man placed the palm of his hand to her forehead, a feeling of warmth running from head to toe. Rae saw a young boy, no older than ten, staring at her. She recognized her surroundings; she was surrounded by chaos at the carnival in the woods. The boy let his fangs drop from his gums and hissed at her before pouncing on her, tackling her to the ground. He dug his fangs into her neck, sucking the life out of her. When she opened her eyes, an elderly man was standing over her, picking her up.

The warmth subsided and she was brought back to the curtained medical room. The doctor had made her lay down and she found herself staring at the murals on the ceiling.

Rae saw cherubs and angels and high arches and pillars. She felt a light shock to her neck where the child had bit her, bringing her to reality.

"Did you know what happened to you, dear?" the old man said.

Rae shook her head, Elijah had told her nothing, just that she needed to rest. She brought her knees to her chest, wrapping her arms around them.

"I don't know why you feel you know me, but I promise you I am not someone to fear. Now, run along dear and I hope you start to feel better soon," he said. He placed a hand on her knee, reassuring her.

When she left, she felt tired, but tried not to let Christine know. Clara led them back through the water door, only this time it opened like normal. The girls looked at each other, confirming they saw the same thing.

"It's a test, something we use to determine whether someone is trustworthy here," Clara said. She had a notebook clasped in her hands in front of her. "It's hard to explain. Some people are drenched with water; others are…shocked and therefore deemed unworthy so to speak."

"I know it doesn't make sense, but we can't have people who delve into the dark arts here in this sanctuary," she continued. "The Elders built this place many centuries ago so that magical beings who have nowhere else to go may come here, and be sheltered by the wards that have been placed on the grounds' borders. Without this place, many of its inhabitants would not be here for one reason or another."

"That's great, Clara, and we really appreciate you bringing us here, but is there any way you can take us back to our friends? We really don't need another history lesson right now," Christine said.

Clara bowed her head, "Of course, right this way Christine."

She led the girls down a corridor with cement pillars on the left side every ten feet holding up the high ceiling. On their right, cobblestone walls with doors every so often formed the other wall.

"This corridor was added on when the school needed to expand. As you can tell, the right side is aged and looks like an exterior wall, whereas the left wall is the interior wall. These pillars lined the exterior of the building many years ago. It wasn't until around 1950 the building needed to be renovated to hold its inhabitants comfortably," Clara explained. "You should see the school from the outside."

Two large double doors stood on the left, leading outside. When Clara opened the doors, a gust of wind filled the room. Her perfectly groomed bob haircut was windswept when she stepped out onto the veranda. Rae and Christine followed, noticing Micah was leaning against a tall white pillar atop a four-foot-tall concrete block.

"It's good to see you, ladies. I hope you are both feeling better," Micah said. His arms were crossed as he leaned against the pillar, his green eyes searching the three women from head to toe. They darted from Christine to Clara and then to Rae, a cute grin on his face.

"How did you get out here?" Clara asked. "I specifically told you to stay inside next to the door of the infirmary."

"Yes, but I got bored, so I decided to look around and I found this beautiful garden!" Micah said, opening his arms toward the yard.

A cobblestone curved driveway met the bottom of the stairs, a large fountain in the center of the curve. A statue of what looked like Benedict was in the center of the fountain surrounded by small children. There were flowerpots along the base of the fountain, adding a little color to the scene. Along the curve of the driveway were large pillars holding up a tall vaulted overhang. The awning reached to the edge of the driveway, ensuring no sun reached the flowerbed around the fountain.

On the other side of the fountain, where the curved driveway led, were two strips of gravel road leading to and from the school. Tall pine trees provided a refreshing scent that relaxed Rae. On either side of the fountain, a radiant garden of tulips and roses, gardenias and geraniums, provided a rainbow of color on the evergreen and bark backdrop of the forest.

Rae and Christine tried to take the stairs down to the fountain but Clara stopped them, putting both her arms straight out to block the girls from leaving the porch.

"This is as far as we go today, you asked me to take you back to your friends, and that is our next stop," Clara said, turning around and prancing into the corridor.

149

She took them straight and then turned down another better-lit corridor with bright paintings on the walls. More doors were apparent down this hallway than were in the other and the girls noticed students walking around, staring at them awkwardly and whispering.

Up a flight of stairs and down another hallway, this time the doors were much closer together and there were only candles on the walls, no paintings, Clara led them to where they would stay for the evening. She opened two doors, one for Rae and one for Christine.

"Here we are," Clara said. "Now rest up. You both have a big day ahead of you tomorrow. Sala and I will be around later this evening to collect you and your friends for supper. But for now, please rest and we shall see you later tonight."

Clara left the girls in their rooms, proceeding to take Micah to his next. His room was on a separate floor, as were most of the male rooms in the Academy. Men and women were separated by floor, not condoning cohabitation. The only times the genders mixed was during training and during meals, if the students decided to dine together.

Micah didn't understand but followed his guide regardless. She knocked on a door, alerting his neighbor of his presence. A tall man with dark brown eyes and blond hair answered the door, looking Micah up and down before speaking.

"Micah will be staying in the room next to you, please introduce yourself and help him out wherever he needs it," Clara interrupted.

"I'm not staying next to a vampire, I'm sorry," the man said.

"You have no choice, considering you're a vampire as well. I'm sure you will have plenty to talk about, Clyde," Clara said, turning to show Micah to his room. "Here is your room and your key. Your friends are across the hall and down a door or two. There are so many of you, but we don't have any rooms to accommodate more than one inhabitant, it's just how the Elders wanted it."

"I don't mind the privacy," Micah said, smiling at her. "Will you be around to collect us this evening?"

Clara nodded, turning to leave, before Micah grabbed her arm. "I hope you know what your Elder is getting into. And everyone needs to prepare for the worst." Micah's breath was hot on her ear as he spoke.

She yanked her arm out of his grip, straightening her skirt before walking away. The vampire Clyde stared at Micah with wide eyes.

"That's right little vampire boy, you heard me. You better sleep with one eye open, you never know what will go bump in the night," Micah chuckled, closing the door behind him.

Chapter 21

Elijah sat on the couch, elbows resting on his thighs, his hands clasped in front of him. He stared at an object on the table, some crystal centerpiece with a wide base the color of coal and four pieces of glass that stretched to the ceiling. One was of a vine, green and brown in color. The second was blue and formed a wave one would surf on with white foam on it. The piece of glass beside that on a corner was shaped like a thin cloud and the final piece was a single red and gold flame. A sphere, gold and white in color, sat inside the glass figure. The centerpiece was only around twelve inches tall, but held so much beauty in it.

Elijah thought about all the simple things that held so much beauty in his eyes. Like the mares grazing in the pasture at his family's estate many years ago, or the drawing he once found of a young couple holding their children, both around the age of two or three. The children were twins, one boy and one girl, who wore peasants clothing. The collars of their blouses were ripped, the man a button or two on his. The children had dirt on their faces, and the girl's hair was tangled. He remembered seeing the drawing by the bedside of Lana when she was staying at the Jacobs' estate to recover after an illness took her strength.

He never asked her about the drawing, mostly because he knew it wasn't his place to ask of her past for she always avoided the subject like the plague. Elijah bowed his head, visions of Lana and of his family surfacing after many years of him subduing them, forgetting any of them ever existed. The air grew cold and Elijah could feel a breeze coming from behind him.

"Don't be alarmed, it's just me," EJ said when Elijah turned around, standing and backing into the glass table. The centerpiece toppled over and rolled off the table, shattering on the ground.

"I knew the couch was too close to the table but you never listen to me," Era said, putting her hands on her hips.

"You know better than to talk to me like that," EJ said, walking down the hallway away from her and Elijah.

"Where have you all been?" Elijah asked, following the Fury.

"Dimitri had Rachel take us to the alternate location," EJ said quietly. "I was sent back to bring you and the girl back with me. Has she woken yet?"

They stopped in front of the door to her room, EJ waiting for an answer before proceeding.

"No, she's still recovering from the last few nights," Elijah answered.

A shriek rang through the hollow hallway, echoing off the walls. Era was pushed into the wall behind her, slumping to the ground, looking up when a man stood over her.

The men snuck into Lana's room before they could see what he would do to EJ's Diviner. Lana was sitting up in bed, spinning a piece of jewelry around her finger when they entered.

"Lana, get dressed quickly, we need to get out of here," EJ said, looking in the closet for any clothing she could put on before their unwelcome guest barged in. He tried to be quiet in an attempt not to alarm the visitor.

Elijah heard footsteps on the other side of the door, a shadow eliminating the light beneath the door. Elijah moved closer to the closet, EJ beside Lana. The doorknob shook, turned, and opened. The room was empty.

EJ and Lana appeared next to Era in the living room, EJ taking her hand. The three disappeared in a white haze before the visitor, a dark-haired man with gray streaks, his hair slicked back with too much hair product, stepped out of the room. Elijah stepped behind the man, placing both hands on either side of his face and snapping his neck.

He stepped over the corpse, walking toward the living room. The man grabbed his ankle, sending a shock through his body. He crumpled to the ground, looking at the man who stood and wiped off his jacket. The man tilted his head from right to left, letting the cartilage crack.

"You really need to be more creative in the way you try to kill people," the man said with a European accent. "It's really quite pathetic."

EJ and the girls stood in the stairwell leading to the basement, listening for any indication of life above them. He placed his index finger to his lips to silence their sobs, their fears. Era's body shook, Lana drew her closer to comfort her. Although she was afraid as well, she knew someone needed to be strong. He left in a cloud of white smoke, leaving the girls defenseless.

"Come out, come out wherever you are!" the Englishman laughed. He had a thick black beard laced with salt colored speckles. Wearing a leather jacket and black motorcycle boots, he walked heavy footed through the living room, flipping tables and slamming chairs against the walls. He knelt to admire the fallen glass sculpture near the couch, taking a variety of colored glass in the palm of his hand.

"Fire," he said as he dropped the orange glass piece. "Water," to the wave. "Air," to the cloud, "Earth," to the vine.

He took the gold sphere in his hand, admiring its pearl facade. He cranked his right arm back and forward, releasing the sphere from his hand. It shattered against the concrete mantle, a velvet covered cube falling to the ground. The velvet was the color of royal indigo, with green vine, red flame, white cloud and blue water drop embroidery decorating the outside of the box.

The man stepped forward, taking the box in his hand. He opened it, only to find it empty. The slit in the foam where a ring would sit had a small indentation within, indicating a ring had once been in the box for many years.

"They found her," he whispered. He felt a cool breeze wash over him, and heard the glass doors from the balcony entrance slam against the wall, shattering on contact. The chandelier above the man jingled and swung back and forth in the wind, the hinges mounted to the ceiling squealing in protest. The bolts shot out from the hinges, letting gravity bring the chandelier toward the floor.

He jumped to the side, rolling over the back of the couch, before the chandelier shattered the glass table.

"Is that the best you've got?" he yelled.

EJ appeared, white dust spiraling around his hands. "Now that you mention it, no."

The glass pieces from the table spiraled into a tornado, sending shards of metal and glass hurtling toward the intruder. He tried to block the attack, rolling to the side. Shards grazed

155

the leather of his jacket, barely damaging the material. The tornado formed back up, sucking in other pieces of debris from the damaged furniture; two splintered pieces of wood from the dining table flew toward him at 50 miles per hour, breaking into pieces on contact with his thigh.

He yelled out in pain, grabbing a piece of the glass door and throwing it toward EJ who tried dodging the wooden projectile. It slid along his shoulder, creating a large gash in his skin. Blood ran down his arm as he lifted his hands to eye level. The dust clouds around his hands formed into icicles, cold and sharp, pointing toward his guest.

"If you kill me, you'll never know what is coming," he said.

"What are you talking about?" EJ asked.

"You think you know, but you are just naive," his guest said. "If you just give us the girl, no one will get hurt."

"Your horde killed 100 innocent people. How can we trust you?" EJ said.

"You can't," the man said. A rod formed in his hand, silver in color with a tip the color of tar. He spun it in his hands, the rod breaking into four pieces. He sent them toward EJ, two of them making contact. One piece punctured his right collarbone, the other his left thigh, the same as the splintered dining table to his enemy.

EJ dropped to his knees, the icicles disappearing. "You won't get away with this," he said.

The man sulked toward EJ, his hand on his thigh. He placed a finger under EJ's chin, forcing the Fury to look him in the eyes. His eyes were pitch black, an image from hell. His face twisted into something EJ had never seen before, with a protruding forehead, high cheekbones, and a small chin. He had a pointed ear on the right side of his face and a burn scar where his left ear should have been.

EJ tried to scream but found his voice gone and mouth dry.

"I've never been this close to your kind," the demon said, his mouth close to EJ's face. His breath was foul, the smell of rotting garbage and burning flesh.

The creature took hold of the rod in EJ's chest, turning it in his hand as he pulled it out. Blood stained his shirt and pooled beneath him on the ground. He placed the rod at the base of his ribs, prepared to end his life.

"How close have you been to death, Fury?" the creature asked, delaying taking EJ's life.

"If you are going to kill me, do it already," EJ said, wincing in pain. He was losing blood faster than he could heal himself and slowly started losing consciousness.

The creature pressed the rod to his skin with slight pressure, breaking the skin. A drop of blood slid down EJ's stomach. He saw something move behind the creature, but before he could say anything, the creature dropped the rod, grabbing at the back of his neck.

Elijah had a tight grip on his prey as he dug his fangs deeper into the creature's neck. The blood was sour and ran black down Elijah's chin, neck, and shirt. The creature grabbed him by the back of the neck, pushing him into the wall. He got back up, grabbing the other splintered leg of the dining table in his left hand. Before the creature could grab him again, he bit into the creature's neck once more, driving the wooden stake through the creature's heart. He felt the blood rush over his hand and the heart pulse fast, and then slow until it no longer beat.

It slumped to the ground, deflating back to the figure of a man with a black beard and too much gel in his hair. Small, black particles started to cover his skin, melting him like he was wax. EJ and Elijah backed away from the creature as it disappeared, leaving nothing but black dust behind.

Elijah came to EJ's side, biting his wrist and putting it near his lips. EJ dismissed the gesture, attempting to stand. He had to lean on Elijah who put his left arm under EJ's right shoulder and around his back to support his weight.

"We have to get the girls," EJ said slowly, slightly distant.

"Where are they?" Elijah asked. When EJ didn't answer, he asked once more, slapping EJ's cheek.

"Basement," EJ said. The two men hobbled to where EJ pointed, Elijah barely fazed by the Fury's inability to keep him upright.

"Lana, Era," Elijah said when they reached the door to the basement.

He heard quick steps on wooden boards and saw a Snow-White blonde woman barge through the door. Her eyes went wide when she saw the appearance of her Fury. When EJ saw Era was safe, he collapsed, his heart rate dropping significantly.

"We have to get him to the academy, Lana he needs your help," Era said.

"The Academy? But I have no idea how to get there," Lana explained.

Era placed her hand on Lana's face, closing her eyes. She saw a large room with tables stacked high with books, a bottle of black ink and a quill on the table. There were windows that stretched from the ground to the ceiling, and long curtains keeping the light out. Lamps illuminated the room, casting dark shadows on the walls. When Era took her hand off Lana's cheek, they both opened their eyes.

"Now, I want you to close your eyes once more, and picture that room. Once you have the picture, nod your head and place your hands out in front of you," Era said slowly. "Elijah, take my hand."

Lana nodded, putting her hands out in front of her.

"Elijah, take her left hand," Era said, and then placed Lana's right hand in EJ's left. She placed her left hand on EJ's chest and looked at Lana. "Now I want you to keep your eyes closed and repeat after me. 'Academy.'"

"Academy," Lana repeated. The four of them were surrounded by a flash of green and blue light.

"Academy," Era said, of which Lana repeated once more. The light got brighter, transporting them away from the house and to another place they had not meant to go.

EJ and Era landed on the floor of a forest, surrounded by pine trees that reached to the sky and cast dark shadows over them, letting no light in from the moon. Elijah and Lana were nowhere to be found. Era stood, dusting pine needles off her clothes.

"Elijah!" she yelled. She heard her name behind her in the distance. "Where are you?"

Elijah sat up, shaking his head. He felt behind his neck, feeling a bump and warm liquid at the base of his neck. He turned around, seeing red liquid on a small rock and a dark headed girl with light gray eyes staring back at him. She sat cross-legged the forest floor, her hands crossed in her lap.

"Are you okay?" Elijah asked. She nodded slowly, but he could see how afraid she was. He could hear her heart racing. Lana had just seen a man she knew nearly dead and managed to take them somewhere they hadn't intended. She could feel herself becoming stronger, and knew one day she would be what they want her to be, but at what cost? When she becomes

Candra, will they take advantage of her powers? Will they be overwhelmed by her power that they turn against her? Become like the Darkness and hunt her down?

She was afraid of becoming a puppet, of someone pulling her strings and of bending to their will because of what she was becoming. Lana was afraid of losing herself.

Elijah stood, helping Lana to her feet before hearing a voice call his name.

"That must be Era," Lana said softly.

"Era?" Elijah yelled back. They walked in the direction of the voice, a question burning their throats. When they saw the Snow-White woman, they rushed to the clearing, kneeling to the ground in case they may be seen.

"Do you know where we are?" Lana asked quietly.

"The Academy is in the middle of a forest. There's no telling in which direction we should travel at this hour of the night," Era said, looking around. The roar of a bear rang through the clearing then, putting Elijah on edge.

"Stay here, I'll see if I can find a trail or find out where that sound came from," he said.

Before the girls could protest, he was gone, exploring the forest floor for signs of life. About a half mile from the girls, he stopped, looking over the edge of a cliff. The drop seemed to be about fifty feet deep, mostly rolling downhill to another clearing with the remnants of a campfire and a small tent made of twigs and leather hide. He made his way back to Lana and Era, taking EJ in his arms.

"There's a drop to the east with a campsite at the bottom. I figure if we can make it down there we can stay for the night and pick up on the search in the morning," Elijah said.

"You need to find the Academy tonight or EJ won't make it through the night," Era said.

"Maybe I can try to transport again? I may be able to get us to the Academy if I concentrate," Lana said. She placed her hand on Era's cheek, begging for a glimpse of the Academy.

Era showed her the garden instead, a large statue of a man in a robe holding an ancient text book in one hand and a wooden walking stick with a gem-like sphere beneath his hand. Surrounding the statue was a bed of flowers, roses, small stepping stones and statues of children dotting the scene. A large cobblestone driveway circled the statue and flowerbed, leading in and out of the compound.

Lana tried to concentrate on the scene, placing her right hand out toward Elijah. Once she knew he was within reach, she took a deep breath in, the word *garden* on the tip of her tongue, and let it out, repeating the process until she could smell the roses in the air. She felt cold stone beneath her, felt the wind on her face. When she opened her eyes, the air escaped her lungs, leaving her breathless.

The image she had seen was no match for what she saw before her. She saw blue forget-me-nots next to lavender and pineapple sage bushes, white and yellow roses next to red and pink tulips. The statue before her stood twenty feet tall made of marble with a copper colored plaque beneath his feet reading *Benedict Jonathan Rinehart, Headmaster, Alucia's Academy of Magical Arts.*

The structure behind him raised four tiers high with four towers topped with spires on each corner of the building. It reminded her of the castle near her homeland at Tarkin's Point with its emerald green flags atop the spires, thick stonewalls, and wooden castle doors leading into the structure. The only modern architecture was a large awning covering the driveway, supported by two large stone pillars. The awning curved with a stained glass window in the archway.

She couldn't help but stare at the beauty before her, surprised she managed to make it to the garden. Era was beside her, holding her hand when Elijah coughed, walking toward the Academy to find help for EJ.

Clara greeted him on the other side of the massive doors, the smile on her face frowning slightly once she saw EJ. They hurried through the halls until they reached the door to the infirmary. When Elijah stepped through the threshold, lightning rained down from the sky, sending a spark of energy through him and forcing him to his knees.

The old healer rushed to them, waving Clara in to grab Elijah and escort him to the other side of the door.

"What was that about?" he asked.

"This is why vampires stay outside of the infirmary," Clara answered, throwing him onto the floor. "The old man should be able to help EJ, but in the meantime, we must get you and the other girls to the dining hall. Your feast awaits."

Chapter 22

A long strand of rectangular tables adorned with bright bouquets of flowers picked from the garden housed a plethora of food ranging from stuffed turkey, pork, and chicken, bowls filled with sweet rolls and butter to the side, casserole dishes harboring green bean and broccoli casseroles with cranberry sauce on each end. The smell of a Thanksgiving feast filled the halls, although November was months away.

Round tables full of students with candles as centerpieces were scattered through the ballroom, three great chandeliers hanging from the vaulted ceiling providing light to the occasion. Champagne glasses were filled with bubbling liquid the color of a lavender bush with dark crystals to keep the liquid cold. On one long wall of the ballroom were tall windows covered by dark green curtains embroidered with a witch's hat, cauldron, and the walking stick the Benedict statue was leaning against.

Opposite the windowed wall stood a stone wall with two tapestries on either side of another round table, this one had a light green table cloth with three seats facing the rest of the hall. Each tapestry was embroidered with the same three symbols and between them on the wall hung a painting of Benedict with his two assistants by his side, Sala on his right and Clara on his left, dressed in fancy gowns and suits from the 1800s as if they were royalty at some point in time.

Once Lana, Elijah, and Era entered the room, Benedict rose from his seat, or rather his throne, raising his glass to toast the evening's meal.

"Finally, we have been waiting for you," the man said in their direction. "As many of you may have heard by now, we have some guests from a not so far away place here in our lovely sanctuary. I ask that you all welcome them into our home, for they are like us and have much to contribute to our cause. To our guests, I hope you have found your way around rather easily, I know this place can be confusing at times, but please don't hesitate to ask another student for guidance if you ever find yourself in a hall you are not familiar with.

"To my dear friend Dimitri, I'm glad we were able to speak earlier today, and if you need anything else from us, please let me know. My Academy is at your disposal, please use our resources as you must and lend a hand when the time comes," Benedict finished.

Dimitri rose, his glass in his hand as well. "I greatly appreciate your generosity, and I thank you kindly for allowing us to stay for a short time. To Benedict, and his tender soul, may we all benefit from it as we continue to make this place a safe haven for others like us."

In unison, each student raised their glass, "Here, here."

Benedict gave a sly grin toward Dimitri, sending a small shiver down his spine. *We just need to convince Aiden to help, and then we will leave this place.* He said to himself.

The men sat down once the others joined Dimitri at his table. Lana sat across from Rae who smiled shyly at her. Beside her, Naida attempted to comfort Era after she explained what had happened to EJ.

"EJ will heal on his own terms, Era," Dimitri said. Elijah clenched his fist, trying to fight the urge to snap at him. "Yes, I understand I said that about Lana, but she did heal, on her own terms, as we Furies often do. You had to wait for her to recover when you found her, because she healed on her own terms. It is times like this where we must step aside and let nature run its course. Do you understand?"

"He understands, but we already lost Lana once…" Micah began to say but let the words hang in the air like smoke drifting away in the wind.

The only sounds in the hall were that of the other students speaking in their cliques while they ate in silence, avoiding eye contact with each other and the question burning in the back of Lana's throat from the time she sat down. One by one, each table rose and exited the room until their table was the only one occupied.

Clara came to their table, cautious of Elijah after she failed to warn him about the lightning.

"Please feel free to stay as long as you would like, but it is time that I show the newcomers to their rooms, per Benedict's request," Clara said.

"I believe it is time for us all to retire for the evening," Dimitri said, standing and placing his napkin over his plate. "Thank you for your help, Clara."

The others stood and followed Clara and Dimitri out of the ballroom and up a grand staircase made of mahogany and a lush light brown carpet. Lana's room was next to Rae's across the hall from the Diviners' and Christine's rooms in Corridor B.

"Here are your keys; I hope you find the rooms to your liking. I designed them myself," she said, speaking highly of

165

herself before turning away and prancing down the hallway like a well-dressed pony.

"Rae," Lana said before she entered her room. "I'm sorry about the party."

"Don't be sorry, you didn't even want to be there. Good night Lana," Rae said, heading into her room and closing the door behind her.

Lana disappeared behind her door, closing and locking it behind her. She flipped on the light switch, a lantern next to the window roaring to life, followed by two candles on the wall around the corner near the bed. There was no light on the ceiling, only candles and natural light from the windows. The curtains were drawn but Lana could make out the color of the velvet curtains to be a scarlet color.

The bed was neatly made with five decorative pillows and a satin robe folded nicely at the edge. To the left of the bed a door led into the bathroom, a small room with a place for a shower and a bowl on top of a cabinet for a sink. A round mirror hung above the sink and three small candles lined the mirror as the source of light.

Across from the bed stood a large armoire for her clothes and belongings with a vanity beside it next to the window. Various belongings scattered the surface of the vanity, a brush, some jewelry, perfume and a picture of a girl with brown hair in two braids with square glasses she recognized as Sala. In between the vanity and the armoire sat a small recliner.

A knock on the door turned her around.

"Here is your bag, we packed what we thought you'd like so you'd have something new to wear," Naida said, handing her a backpack.

"Thank you," Lana said. "Why are we here?"

"I can't answer that, have a good night," Naida said. She disappeared in a cloud of smoke.

The water was warm on her skin as she washed off the events of the last few days. She didn't know how long it'd been since the party, but she could tell it could only have been a few days with how sore her body felt. Lifting her arms to wash her hair was a task; even getting dressed took longer than usual.

She pulled back the sheets, sliding between them before pulling them to her chin. She stared at the dark ceiling, wondering what the outcome of the party had truly been. She wondered if Aiden showed up, and if he had, whether he had been harmed.

Aiden.

She hadn't thought of a man since she left Clover Bay in 1840, since she had been betrayed by Micah, by the ones she once called her friends. But something about Aiden made her *want* to think about a man, about *him.*

Lana remembered what he had said at the bonfire, that he didn't want a relationship with Christine because she was clingy and that Lana calmed him when she was around. She shook the thought away, feeling bubbles swim through her stomach like when Micah first confronted her of feeling for another, other than herself. Turning on her side, she closed her eyes, hoping sleep would come quickly.

~

A figure the shape of a man covered in lava rock and flames stood above her, his eyes the color and consistency of molten lava, a bright orange she could feel burning into her skin. She screamed as the figure bent down to grab hold of her.

She felt a pressure on her shoulders and heard her name in the distance.

"Lana," Dimitri said, shaking her shoulders lightly. "Lana, wake up."

She woke, covered in sweat, tendrils of hair stuck to her cheeks and forehead. "How did you get in here?"

"You haven't learned anything, have you?" he chuckled. "What were you dreaming about?"

"You call that a dream?" she asked, realizing how rude she sounded after the fact. "Some fire demon…"

Dimitri broke eye contact with her then, unsure what she knew of the night Aiden found her in the woods.

"So, what are you doing here?" she asked him.

"I wanted to speak with you this morning and answer any questions you might have, if you would like?" Dimitri said.

"Why are we here at this place?" she asked.

"Do you remember we spoke of the Darkness when we began your training? Well, they have found you, and now we are here to throw them off regarding your whereabouts," he explained. "This place, it is a sanctuary for people like us. If we were to stay here for longer than I intend, you would be able to learn more about faeries, witches, vampires, shape shifters, you name it. Benedict watches over them here. He founded this place and was able to find all these beings who needed his protection from the mundane, from people who wanted to turn them into lab rats."

"I chose this place to bring you to, because of his ability to not only protect us but also train Christine and Rachel in the unfortunate event that we need their abilities. This place is the perfect training ground for you to master what we have already taught you…" he paused, thinking of Aiden, the last piece of the puzzle to unlock her powers. "And what we have yet to teach you. You will learn much more in our time here. That I am sure of."

"What else must I learn?"

"Are you afraid of fire?" Dimitri asked.

~

Lana followed Dimitri into the study, the large room Era showed her the first time she tried to transport them to the Academy. Much like the garden, this room was much grander compared to the image she saw from Era. With a gigantic chandelier hanging from a vaulted ceiling, the images of cherubs, angels, horned beings, and decorative swirls painted on the extensive canvas, large windows whose curtains were drawn back to fill the room with natural light, a wall full of bookshelves, full of books and scrolls on the wall opposite the windows, and a long rectangular desk stacked high with books, scrolls and a map of the compound atop it.

On the other side of the desk stood Wiley, indicating she would be learning more about Earth and Water, two of her primary elemental powers. Her mind darted to EJ and how his recovery was going; Wind was one of the elements she felt she could improve on.

"What are your feelings toward what you are?" Dimitri asked.

"I feel like I haven't been told what my role in all of this is," she answered.

"Each of us has a role. Wiley and I are here to instruct you on how to tap into each element of which you are in control of, or can be in control of. EJ, when he returns, will also be here to instruct you on his power," Dimitri said. "Each element you master brings you closer to mastering your true power. But first, you have to be comfortable enough with what you have been taught before we can proceed with your training."

"In the coming days, we will test you on what you have learned, and if you fail, you will redo those lessons you once completed," Wiley said. "If you feel like you can proceed to the next lesson, you will not until we feel you can do so. It will be rough; you remember what it was like the first time we found you, and it will be that way once more. In fact, it will be much worse. We will be fitting months' worth of training in days due to the primary fact that the Darkness is on its way. For all we know, they could already be here."

"First, we will begin with the essentials, balance," Dimitri said, taking a few steps toward Lana. He placed his hand on her shoulder, the two leaving the study to head into the forest.

~

Splintered wood, shattered glass, fallen chandeliers, and broken doors were all he could see when he entered the clubhouse. Blood near the balcony doors and a broken table leg covered in dried liquid set his senses ablaze. He could feel himself losing his grip on the calm he'd tried to obtain overnight. The last few days destroyed the walls he spent centuries building, dedicated everything he had to patching up the holes of his past.

He knelt beside the drying puddle of blood, examining the pile of black dust only inches away. Seeing a shimmer beneath the ash, he reached, feeling the cool metal of a ring.

EJ's ring. The diamond shone in the light, a cloud embellished on the side of the ring. Aiden dropped to his knees and let out a yell, or rather a roar. His hands erupted in flames, his eyes the color of lava. He placed them on the ground, sending bolts of fire to anything flammable. The flames started to spread until the entire living room was engulfed in them.

Red, orange, gold, blue, green, and white flames raced up walls, on the ceiling, down hallways and into rooms. He followed them down hallways, running his hands along the walls until he was facing the painting made centuries before. He stared at the faces, from his to Dimitri, Wiley, and EJ.

They were brothers, bound to one another through the power of the Fury, through the devastation of their homeland and the beginning of an end. He knew this time would be different, that this time they may lose their lives if the Light couldn't find them this time around.

He'd wanted to burn the painting the day Dimitri hung it on the wall but today, today it would be the only thing he didn't burn in the house. He took the large framed canvas in his hands, admiring the art before him. He would save these men if it meant laying his life down for them, that he was absolutely certain of.

Aiden took the painting, leaving the burning clubhouse behind as the Darkness closed in on his position. He gave nothing away, and let the past burn.

Chapter 23

The sound of rushing water could be heard through the forest, over the crunch of twigs beneath their feet, the birds chirping and leaves rustling in the wind. They stood on the edge of a precipice at the base of a large tree that had been uprooted when the ground collapsed around it. The trunk of the tree extended forty feet over the gorge, attached only by the roots begging to break.

"You expect me to walk on that thing?" Lana asked.

"Yes. You must learn how to balance. You are tasked with balancing on that tree trunk, all while we test how well you can block out what we throw at you," Dimitri said calmly. She saw the leaves turn brown and fall off their branches toward the now dry riverbed beneath.

The only obstacles she could see them conjuring would be to flood the canyon or create a rain storm, maybe even shrink the trunk of the tree, leaving her to balance atop a thin branch.

She walked around the roots, finding a place to climb onto the dying tree trunk. She knew it would be difficult but if she didn't succeed, she could never stand a chance against the Darkness chasing after her. Her hands gripped the rough bark as she crawled toward a thinner part of the tree.

Lana released the bark, wiping brown flakes from her hands, her nerves causing her entire body to shake. She knew they wouldn't let her fall, but she still feared heights, and the fact that she no longer heard water beneath her, made her even more afraid. There would be no soft landing if she were to fall.

She placed one foot in front of the other, slowly raising her upper body and straightening her legs until she stood straight. Her toes curled in her shoes while she tried to get a better grip on the trunk.

Small teardrops dotted her cheeks, pelting the leaves above her. She knew this had to be Wiley and his obstacle. A rain shower. Lana could smell the dirt in the air; feel the moisture trying to flood her concentration. She closed her eyes, taking a deep breath in through her nose and out through her mouth. Slowly, the vibration through her dwindled until she was no longer shivering.

Lana felt more raindrops on her cheeks, her arms, felt the cool liquid on her scalp. The tempo of the rain picked up, covering the Furies from head to toe. When she opened her eyes, she could see only the gray of the downpour. Although EJ was not around to blow the rain around, she started to feel cold, the rain cooling the forest down ten degrees.

Dimitri was right, the rain did break her concentration. She started shaking again when she heard the rush of water beneath her once more.

"Concentrate, Lana," she thought she heard Dimitri say but it was too late, the water had risen to greet her ankles, then her knees until she was surrounded by the river. He looked at his partner who released the rain, letting the river subside until the branch was visible.

Lana fell hard on the tree trunk, her feet slipping out from under her. She rolled over the edge of the trunk, plummeting toward the draining riverbed. She was met by a spider web of vines in the shape of a bridge from one side of the chasm to the other. When she landed, Dimitri stood before her.

"Is that the best you can do?" he said, kneeling in front of her when she sat up.

"That's not fair. He practically tried to drown me…" she said.

"You have to learn how to ignore what is happening around you. Instead of concentrating on standing on the tree trunk once you felt the water, you should have let it take you for a ride. Or you could have counteracted his power with your own."

"I can't be what you want me to be, can't you see that?"

"You are capable of so much more than you believe, Lana. I've seen what you can do with your power, I've seen the damage your power can do. All you have to do is look deep inside and harness it."

"I've already done this balancing act before, why do I have to do it again?"

"Because we haven't worked with you in many years, and we want to ensure you have full control over your powers before we have to fight whatever they throw at us next. In order to do that, we have to start from the beginning…"

"But we don't have time to start from the beginning!" she yelled, feeling a surge of energy run through her. They stood in unison, Lana trying to calm her mind. She wanted to emulate Wiley's flood, his rainstorm, let buckets of water fall from the clouds above. She pictured white and then gray and dark blue clouds form above the tops of the pine trees, bursts of light fill the sky. She felt gusts of wind pick Dimitri's vine bridge up from below, sending her stomach up and down.

"Concentrate."

174

At that, white and brown water formed a wave against one wall of the canyon, raining down on them.

"I know you are frustrated, but taking your frustrations out on me will get you nowhere," Dimitri said. In his eyes, she saw the reflection of her creation. "Concentrate on your breathing, in and out."

She closed her eyes, letting the wind whip her hair around her face. She did as he said, breathing in through her nose and out multiple times. The wave behind her stood ten feet tall, towering over her. She could still hear it behind her, although it started to swim down the mountainside, flowing over the river rocks until it calmed to a slow flow downhill.

A tear escaped down her cheek, Dimitri wiping it away.

"It won't be this difficult for long. This is what you get for running away," he said. The two joined Wiley at the edge of the canyon, heading back through the trees toward the Academy.

~

The unfamiliar vibration of cobblestones beneath his tires surfaced when he turned into her driveway. A blue Mercedes sat feet from him, Professor Thomas walking toward it with his hands in his pockets.

"What are you doing here?" Aiden asked, his jaw clenching.

"Just checking on Miss McDowall, which I assume you are here for the same reasons," Professor Thomas answered.

Aiden nodded, mimicking his body language. "Why? After what you did to her."

"What are you talking about?"

"I saw the bruises on her neck," Aiden said. "After what you did, why would someone like you personally come check up on her?"

"I don't know what you're talking about," Professor Thomas stated. "I would never hurt Lana. She isn't home, so I'll be off. Have a good night, Aiden."

Professor Thomas got in his car and drove away, looking back toward the house before speeding down the street. Aiden stood staring at the front door.

Aiden peered through the stained glass, getting a glimpse of a marble floor. He transported into the foyer, staring at himself in the mirror and looking around for a light. He didn't know if anyone was in the home, so he snapped his fingers instead, a small ball of flame forming in his hand. The doors to the living room were open, giving him access to the vast space of which a fire had consumed. There were pieces of vases scattered across the room, and what remained of the leather of the couches was torn open with the foam insulation littering the floor like cotton candy.

Aiden perused the area, searching for blood or worse, but found nothing, not even dust, an identifier that the Darkness had been there. He was careful not to step on any glass, in case someone was in the mansion. That's when he heard it.

A loud thud rang through the house, like someone fell or dropped something the equivalent of a statue on the second floor. Floorboards creaked above him, dust falling through the cracks of the ceiling. He looked around for a place to hide, coming up short. He heard footsteps on the stairwell, found a book on the ground to look busy and on the window seat when the intruder came into the room.

A young man in a red and white letterman's jacket and jeans walked in, an old textbook in his hand. When he saw

Aiden, he stuck his left hand in his pocket, wiggling his ring off.

"How can I help you?" the man asked.

"I'm not looking for help, thank you though," Aiden said, pretending to be engrossed in *The Great Gatsby*.

"Then I'm afraid I'm going to have to ask you to leave. This home is for people who need it, not for casual coming and going," he said.

"What would I need to stay?" Aiden asked.

"Why are you here?" the man returned.

"I came to see a friend, but they don't seem to be here. I'm sorry I bothered you," Aiden said. He put the book down on the seat, heading toward the man to leave.

"What's your name?" the man asked.

"I could ask you the same thing, sir," he said.

"Don, you?"

"Aiden," he held out his hand to shake Don's but the man refused, keeping his hand in his pocket. "Have a good day, Don."

He left the room, pulling out his phone the minute he closed the door to his truck.

Hey D, something isn't right here. Where are you guys? – A

...

We've gone to the Academy, I suggest you get out of the Bay while you can. It is not safe for our kind. – D

...

I need to make sure Lana is safe first, where did you guys take her? – A

...

Just come to the Academy. Lana is safe. – D

Aiden didn't respond, afraid he'd be angry with Dimitri for keeping him in the dark. He didn't like the thought of not knowing where she was, not with this Don character hiding out in her house. What did he mean by 'this home is for people who need it?'

He remembered catching a glimpse at the textbook in his hand, a book of spells it seemed. The cover was leather with old parchment paper bound with twine. The spine had a pentagram, symbolizing the textbook was meant for witches. The pentagram symbolizes the four elements, plus a pantheistic spiritual being such as Gaia or Mother Earth.

Why would Lana have a book like that in her home? He had many questions for her, questions he truly did not want the answers to. He desperately hoped she was normal, that Dimitri was lying and she was a human that he could pretend to be human with, but everything he had experienced lately pointed in the direction of witchcraft.

He put the truck in drive, leaving Lana's home behind. He drove through town, stopping in the parking lot of the school. Looking around to make sure no one was watching he left the vehicle, bypassing locked doors until he was in the art room. He grabbed his journal from the cabinet, searching through the other names until he found Lana's.

Professor Baldwin came around the corner as he started digging through her cabinet.

"Aiden? What are you doing here so late on a weekend?" she asked sweetly.

"I left my sketchbook," he answered. "I didn't realize you were in here."

"I didn't hear the door open," she said curiously. "I haven't seen you in my class lately."

"My family has been having problems," Aiden said. He didn't know where she was going with the conversation, or how to get out of it.

"Well please let Dimitri know that I would like to speak with him," Professor Baldwin said. "I'm not like the rest of the teachers here, Aiden. I would think you of all people would know by now, considering I know about the lake, and about you."

"How long have you known?"

"Since you came here, dear. It's the beauty of being a psychic. Now that the lake incident has been taken care of, you need to watch your back. Members of the Darkness are starting to come into the school, pretending to be students so they can create a presence here. I vowed to protect those who come into the school who have abilities like you and I but this I cannot protect you from," she explained.

"Have you come across a man named Don yet?" Aiden asked.

She pursed her lips, the skin between her eyebrows squeezing together. She shook her head, not recognizing the name.

"When you do let me know, I ran into him today and he gave me an odd feeling. I'm heading out to find the others, and I'll keep in touch," he said.

"Have you seen Lana?" she asked, hesitant at first. Aiden stopped and turned slowly, confused.

"Not since the lake," Aiden said.

Professor Baldwin knew then that Aiden didn't know what Lana was, and she tried to backtrack to keep him from figuring out she was in danger.

"If I see her I'll let you know."

She smiled when he turned to walk out of the room. Why would Professor Baldwin ask about Lana if she was a Psychic? Unless she knew something Aiden didn't? He didn't want to think about her as anything but human. He couldn't think of her as anything but that. He left his truck in the parking lot, heading straight for the Academy while he knew no one could follow.

Chapter 24

Lana sat on the divan near the window in the library of the Academy, reading over pieces of parchment decorated with images and small phrases. One depicted a large hall with more than twenty tall columns to support its vaulted ceiling. Every five pillars a vast chandelier with candles lit the hall and tables draped with crimson colored material scattered the area between the pillars and the walls.

In between the pillars, a four-foot wide violet carpet with thick gold edges ran from the large double doors entering the hall to the steps that led to a tall-backed gold and black thrown. She read the caption beneath the illustration: *Kimar's throne, the hall of the Greats.*

Each image was beautifully sketched yet held no true information regarding them. She pictured the hall in her head, a plump king sitting on his throne, women in puffy dresses holding hands with men in tunics and riding boots dancing down the center of the hall. Some people dined at the tables between pillars and walls. She felt pressure on her shoulder, shaking her from the past.

"Are you ready for your next lesson?" Dimitri asked.

"Tell me the story of the Fury," Lana said sternly.

"That is for another time," he dismissed.

"Why can't you tell me now?"

"Because the past is not important, what is important is that we strengthen your skills to ensure a successful outcome when we are pitted against the Darkness," Dimitri said flatly.

"Why are you so confident we'll succeed? Did you happen to see what happened to the previous Light Fury when he went up against the Darkness?" Lana pried.

"The previous Light Fury was a woman, and no I did not," Dimitri said, his voice haunted by grief. "However, that is beside the point. My point is that you are much more powerful than you give yourself credit for. You just need to learn how to control it. I believe that with practice, you will be able to not only defeat the Darkness, but survive to live a long, prosperous life."

"So, you never saw what happened to them? Clearly, they didn't survive, otherwise I wouldn't be here," she tried to stay level-headed, but she could not control the wind from forcing the bay windows open, the latch which held them closed swaying from left to right.

"They could have survived, and died later on from unknown causes," Dimitri said calmly.

"How can you be so certain that I'll survive if you can't be sure how they died?"

"That is enough," Dimitri yelled, his voice booming through the study. The wind died down until the windows shut. He walked over and slid the clasp into the D-ring to secure them. "Sit down, and I'll tell you the story."

He took a seat across from her on the scarlet velvet, placing his hands on his lap neatly. He clasped them together, closing his eyes. With a sigh, he opened them, the light green iris glowed a dull yellow.

"During the month of April in 1452, the cherry blossom trees began blooming. There was a strong rose-like aroma in the air whenever we stepped outside. Blossoms of every color seemed to grow all around. The Alucia woods, they were always a beautiful blue-purple color and when you were beneath the pines the sun seemed to glow a bright pink color. As amazing as the Alucia woods were, nothing compared the beauty of the cherry blossoms. There was this festival the king would host whenever they were in bloom. So many people from all walks of life would attend, even people who would be affiliated with the Darkness.

"Of course, we all knew who we were then, but these creatures never seemed to cause any trouble in the past. When Arin arrived for the festivities, the Darkness started causing trouble. Some of their vampires would take villagers and drain them, leaving them in the streets. They started causing hysteria, people went missing, other creatures we had taken in and protected from them to be exact. Arin tried to explain what was coming, seeing as how we were still very young and inexperienced when it came to using our power.

"However, we were not inexperienced in battle. She explained what we'd already suspected, that the Darkness had found its way into our lives and was threatening to tear our world apart. Our human villagers became ill, spreading a deadly plague throughout the land. Kingdoms, villages, small farming towns all came in search of aid and protection but we were not equipped to fight what came next.

"Whenever we found the Diviner's they claimed they had been exiled from a kingdom known to practice dark magic," Dimitri paused. "Terra was the one with whom I spoke with frequently. She assured me they were harmless, although they were creatures who were famous for their illusions. When they'd proved themselves worthy of freedom, they clung to us, their saviors. Leressi, you've had an encounter with her, have you not? Well she was different, and she had trouble integrating into our society. It wasn't until the festival that we saw who she really was.

"She'd betrayed us, calling the Darkness once she knew Arin was among us," Dimitri sighed. "Screams broke out in the streets, demons, vampires, dark witches; any evil creature you could imagine swarmed the village. Before we could do anything, Arin had already been captured. Julius, a good friend of the king's, had been the one to take her, dispatching horsemen to find and kill anyone affiliated with not only the king but us as well. He made everyone believe we were not to be trusted, that we had lied and used the humans and other creatures and that we needed to pay.

"We chased him down but Benedict caught us before we could reach Julius, leading us away from the real battle and up to safe ground. EJ and I had been separated from Wiley, who had gone to find the Diviners," Dimitri paused, seeing the questions bubbling in Lana's eyes.

"How does Aiden fit into all of this?" Lana asked.

The double doors separated then, Aiden pushing them open. Dimitri stood, putting him between the Ruby Fury and her.

"What have you told her?" Lana could hear the anger in his voice.

"The truth," Dimitri said.

"She doesn't need to know about this world, Dimitri. She's a human, and humans have no business playing with magic they do not understand," Aiden said. Lana could see a small ring of orange dancing around his pupil. She gasped, placing her hand over her mouth.

"Aiden calm down, this is not the time for your temper to get the best of you," Dimitri said calmly. Lana knew story time was over, and her training regarding the element of fire would begin soon. "Lana has something to tell you."

"I'm taking her home, Dimitri," Aiden pushed Dimitri aside.

"No, you're not," Lana said, trying to keep her voice steady.

"You don't understand the kind of danger you're in if you stay here," he said, kneeling next to her. The glowing ring had disappeared as he tried to seem as normal as he could around her.

"Go ahead Lana, tell him," Dimitri said, clasping his hands behind him.

"I'm not human," Lana stumbled over the words, her voice cracking. She had refused to look at him when he came near her, afraid of what she'd see.

"I don't understand," Aiden said. She played with the ring on her finger, spinning it around. He saw the amethyst gemstone sparkle in the light from the window, the heat rushing to his cheeks. He turned on Dimitri, flames dancing in his irises. "Why did you not tell me what she was? You let me believe she was human?"

"I told you at the club house but you had that belief from the moment you met her, Aiden. No amount of my trying to educate you on our find would change that," Dimitri said. "We found her many years ago, and you were nowhere to be found, so why would we disrupt your vacation?"

"You really think I would have been angry had you told me what you'd found?" Aiden laughed.

"Yes, considering how you're acting now," Dimitri said. "Here's the best part, Aiden. You get to train her. Your power is the only one she has yet to master. I hope you can get over yourself long enough to prepare her for what is to come, because otherwise we will ultimately be destroyed."

Aiden started to turn away when he saw a white puff of smoke behind Dimitri. Lana had left the Academy, and they had little to no idea where she would go.

Lana found herself in the entryway to her home, staring at herself in the mirror. Water stained her cheeks, dark circles formed beneath her eyes and her normally curled hair fell flat down her back. She headed into the living area, stepping over broken porcelain, couch stuffing, and burnt floorboards. Before she reached the kitchen, she paused, turning around to face the fireplace. She was being watched, seeing black as she hit the floor.

The wood felt cool against her cheek, feeling a faint wind fall over her. She blinked, the room coming into focus. Black and white Converse sneakers were a foot from her face, a magazine as a makeshift fan held by the intruder in her home. She saw his lips moving but couldn't make out his words. They were muffled, like water had been stuck in her ears. Lana tried focusing on his face but blinked multiple times, the image never sharpening. She rolled onto her back, rubbing her eyes with the palm of her hands.

She left her hands over them, the image of a wooden home with a straw roof and twigs strewn together as a makeshift door. The only lights in the room were of candles, illuminating the features of a bucket for a sink filled with dirty water, and two long wooden planks with straw and blankets for beds.

Lana sat on the plank behind her, reaching into the bucket for the rag she left the morning before. A shiny dinner plate leaned up against the back wall of the hut doubled as a mirror. She caught herself staring at her reflection revealing her shoulder length hair pulled back with a piece of twine, her gray eyes were tired and drooping slightly. Candles illuminated the small room, casting dark shadows on the left side of their mother's face, beads of sweat dotting her forehead. She wrung the water from the rag, placing it on the pale woman's skin.

"You have always been so good at taking care of people," she croaked. "You will make a wonderful bride someday, Aleana."

"The doctor said you just needed rest," Aleana whispered. "You can't leave us…"

Donovan etched away at a dull knife with a rock, the scraping distracting her. She looked over at him, dark shadows on the right side of his face shielding his features – cheekbones identical to hers, plump lips, and a small ball for a nose with a thin bridge and dark brown eyes. His hair was in his face, a black color and matted.

"The doctor was wrong," he said. "There is nothing left to do but let her go in peace."

"Go with your brother, my daughter. Be free of this place," her mother coughed. With a bony hand, she traced Aleana's cheekbones to her jaw line, turning her head to the left.

Her mother's voice turned into a whisper, forcing her to place her ear closer to her mother's mouth. The only words she could make out were 'meet again' before her mother let out a long breath, her eyes glazing over with death. Lana inhaled deeply, sitting up and pushing herself away from him. She looked at his face, hoping her memory would aid in sharpening the image before her. Luckily, she could make out his features. The cheekbones, jaw line, even dark eyes. She began to shake, mumbling the words.

"You're supposed to…be dead," she said breathlessly.

"Calm down, Lana," he spoke clearly then, walking like a duck toward her. He put his knees to the ground, then his palms.

"No don't come near me," she shrieked.

"Don't be afraid, I'm not here to hurt you," he said.

"How did you…"

"Survive? I could ask you the same thing, Aleana," he said.

"That's not my name," Lana said, her voice wavering.

"And Donovan is not mine either," he said, a smile forming on his face. His lips curled back but no fangs dropped. He was not a vampire.

"What are you?" she asked, afraid of the answer.

"Already jumping right into the water, I see," Donovan said.

"Get out of my house before I call the police," Lana said, finding the strength to stand. She braced herself against the small end table against the wall, keeping a wary eye on her brother.

"You really should be sitting down, you took quite a hit. I think you even dented the hard wood," he said, looking at the floor and then back at her. He stood as well, towering over here by almost a foot.

"And you really should be leaving," she broke eye contact.

"You look tired, sister. Why don't I carry you to bed? Maybe we can talk more in the morning?" he offered.

"Apparently you're deaf. Get out of my house!" she pointed in the direction of the front door, her voice cracking as she spoke. "You're dead to me, Donovan."

His facial expressions once held concern, then humor, but twisted to disgust. He took two steps toward her, looking down into her young features. She hadn't aged a day since they'd last seen each other the evening her mother died.

"You never were one for manners, Aleana. I'd think twice before speaking to me in that tone, it may do more harm than good," Donovan said. His breath was hot on her face as she stared at his chest, refusing to play his game. "Good night, sister, I hope we meet again."

"Wait," Lana called after him, the man stopping in the doorway. "He said your name in the woods…"

"Who?"

"I don't know his name, but he said you would be pleased he found me."

Donovan looked back at his sister. "It can't be…"

Lana swallowed hard, clenching and unclenching her fists. "Please tell me it isn't true."

He returned to his original place in the living room, taking her left hand. He turned it over, revealing the amethyst ring. Placing his left hand in his pocket, he replaced the ring and showed her his hand.

"We're…"

"Supposed to kill each other…" Lana finished his sentence, her voice shaky. Tears stained her cheeks, her brother reaching up. On instinct, she flinched. Last time he raised his hand to her, she bruised. He always said he was preparing her for the attack, making her stronger so she would survive. No amount of her repeating those words in her head after he left forgave him for the abuse he inflicted.

"I never found you, got it? We don't know what the other is, do you understand?" Donovan's voice was frantic, his hands clasping around her wrists hard. "You can't tell anybody you know who I am, what I am or question what we're supposed to do."

"Donovan, I'm scared."

"We will figure this out, do you understand? This isn't what we're supposed to be, supposed to do."

"But the prophecy…"

"Screw the damn prophecy. You're my sister. I can't…"

"Donovan, don't leave me again," Lana cried. He shook his head and was gone in a matter of seconds, racing out the front door and into the woods. She collapsed on the floor, hugging her knees to her chest. Visions of her past life came like a flood, drowning her in her own tears. She saw her mother's glossy eyes, the way Donovan stood guard at their door when they'd heard screams resonating through the village. He looked toward her with eyes that said goodbye, throwing the door open and disappearing into the fog. Fire and smoke choked her out of the small house, forcing her to seek lower ground.

She'd found a horse but was pulled off it the moment she mounted. She found herself fighting back against a large man with gray hair and white eyes. Before he had the chance to slit her throat, a man with blond hair cut his head off, reaching a hand toward her. He pulled her onto his horse, riding off into the forest and leaving the burning village behind.

The next vision Lana had, she was raiding villages with Roderick, a childhood friend who'd saved her from the man threatening her life. He taught her how to shoot with bows and arrows and how to hunt. They'd been traveling at night through the forest from town to town, stealing food and supplies to survive. Roderick made camp while Lana found a nearby river to clean up in, but he was gone when she made her way back to the camp. She tracked the headhunters down, unable to free Roderick before they beheaded him in return for what he had done to their men weeks prior.

She'd changed her appearance, her name, started a new life in a town named Aramore. There she was a tailor who'd make dresses and tunics for the local townsfolk. The headhunters hadn't thought to look there. She'd cut her hair short and stayed behind closed doors, only traveling out of her home for supplies, most of which were brought to her door.

Years later, Lana turned up on a small dirt road during a cold, rainy evening in 1840. She'd been traveling for months without food or water, trying to find a way to end her nomadic life, but nothing had seemed to kill her. For almost two centuries she'd lived, unable to fall ill, become fatally wounded, die of her own volition or even at the hand of another. She had no family or friends, and had lost hope that she'd never find out who she really was.

Exhausted and starved, Lana lay on the side of the road wrapped in a thin blanket. A horse drawn carriage pulled up, a man with brown hair and jade green eyes coming to her side. She was unconscious and developing a mild case of hypothermia. She woke up in a bed with a man named Elijah by her side, telling her she was ill and needed to rest. Lana met the love of her life minutes later, finding more than one reason to attempt another try at having a normal life.

Lana shook herself from her devastated and lonely past to find herself rocking back and forth on the floor in her living room. She'd cried so much her eyes were dry and sore, the liquid sticking strands of hair to her cheeks. She'd never thought she'd see her brother again the night he'd left her alone in the village, and she hated him for never finding her. She wondered why it took him so long to search for her, but didn't want to hear the answer.

She imagined the art room, Aiden sitting on a stool on the stage with his torso exposed to all the fantasizing girls, hating that she had to imagine a scene with him in it for her to go there. When she looked around the room at the easels and desks torn to pieces and paint splattered along the walls and floors she stood quickly, hoping nothing bad had fallen upon Professor Baldwin.

The Fury took cautious steps around the room, making sure to leave it the way she'd found it. The door hung off its hinges, a black dust leading to the outer square. Instead of following the path, she continued to search the art room for signs of Ms. Baldwin, failing. She went to the cabinets, locating Aiden's cubby. She looked inside, finding a place where something had recently been taken out. The amount of dust hanging around the thin clean space suggested the sketchbook had collected the small particles gradually over time and was rarely removed from its hiding place.

She heard something drop behind her, too startled to turn around.

Lana, don't move, she heard in her head. It was Professor Thomas.

Kyle? You're supposed to be dead...

She had the urge to disobey him, wondering if it was him she'd heard in the room or someone else. Lana slowly turned around, seeing Professor Baldwin standing in the center of her art room. Professor Thomas was nowhere to be found, only her art teacher with eyes as dark as night.

She tilted her head to the right, pulling her lips back in a tight smirk, revealing black rotting teeth. Before Lana could imagine being in another place, Professor Baldwin sprung onto her, opening her mouth wide Lana heard her jaw crack, seeing a black smoke start to funnel out of the Psychic's mouth.

A hand clamped over the opening, the smell of burning flesh tickling her nose. Professor Thomas wrapped his free arm around Professor Baldwin, pulling her off Lana. She ran for the door, feeling claws dig into her back. Letting out a scream she whirled around, swinging her left arm at the creature behind her. She threw her entire body onto Professor Baldwin, wrapping her fingers around her throat.

Professor Thomas began mumbling another language, banishing the demon within the teacher. When it refused to release Professor Baldwin, Lana placed her hand on her teacher's chest, concentrating on the demon within. She curled her fingers into her palm, forming a fist and pulled her hand away, grabbing hold of a sheer spirit. Professor Thomas grabbed it from Lana, driving a silver-plated stake through it. It disintegrated into black dust.

Professor Baldwin looked at the two of them, dazed at the evening's events. They pulled her to her feet, sitting her down in the only chair that hadn't been harmed during the intrusion.

"Thank god you weren't here when they came," she said.

"Who came for you?" Professor Thomas asked.

"Not for me, for her," Professor Baldwin answered. "Lana, you have to get out of Clover Bay. You have to go back to the others; they are your only hope."

"I'm not leaving you here after what has happened. Come with me, Josephine," Lana begged.

"I'm afraid it's too late for that, my dear," she said, running a cool hand through Lana's hair. "Professor Thomas will accompany you, won't you Kyle?"

"If we are to leave, we must go now before they come back. They'll know something isn't right here and we can't risk you being out in the open," Professor Thomas said. As much as she didn't want to go anywhere with him, they both had a point. After her encounter with Donovan and the

Darkness attacking the closest thing she ever had to a mother, she had no choice but to go back to the Academy.

"Aiden asked about some man named Don. Was he talking about Donovan?" Josephine asked.

"When did he run into Donovan?" Lana asked.

"Before he left to find the others," Josephine said. "Who is he?"

"He's my brother," she said softly. Professor Thomas grabbed hold of her arm, his fingertips placed against her temple. He showed her a studio apartment with the bare necessities. It had a recliner, television, small bed and a kitchenette.

She imagined them within it, taking them to the tiny white room. He quickly made himself busy grabbing some clothes, a few daggers, some stakes, and a crossbow. He placed them all in a bag, brushing past Lana.

"Why are you here? You're supposed to be dead." Lana asked.

"Do you need anything from your house?" Mr. Thomas said.

"Demons know where I live, I can't go back there, not with Donovan running around the Bay," she answered.

He took her hand, grabbing his bag. She imagined the study, the large bay windows and double doors Aiden had pushed open in frustration at finding her in the Academy. She pictured herself perched on the divan in the corner, looking over illustrations and begging Dimitri to tell her the story of the Crusade. The two disappeared in a cloud of smoke, landing hard on the floor of the study.

The doors had been closed and the lights blown out. The curtains had been drawn, letting no light, if any existed, in from outside. Professor Thomas cursed beneath his breath, standing and brushing himself off. He extended a hand to Lana who refused, pushing herself off the ground.

"How are you still alive? I burned your bones," she asked.

"That trick? It only kills the demon hunter, not the warlock," Professor Thomas said. "Thank you, by the way. I haven't felt this alive in years."

"Do you even know why I did it?"

"Because of the demon, I know."

Lana wanted to ask more questions, but was more worried about Professor Baldwin.

"Is she going to be ok?"

"That I can't discuss with you, but I can tell you that she has served her purpose, and anything that happens after this is out of our control," Professor Thomas said, examining the study.

The double doors opened once more, Dimitri, Benedict, and Aiden entering together discussing how they were going to go about finding Lana. They stopped quickly, eyeing the Amethyst Fury and her guest.

"Before you say anything, now is not the time to lecture her," Professor Thomas said, putting himself between the other Furies and the Academy headmaster.

Aiden launched himself at Professor Thomas, flames engulfing his fists. They collided with the warlock's face, bruising and burning his skin.

"What are you doing here?" Aiden asked, lifting his fist from another blow.

"Something has happened in the Bay," he said, pausing when he felt Lana intruding into his thoughts.

Don't tell him.

"Professor Baldwin was attacked and possessed by a demon. When I found her, she was wrestling with Lana," Professor Thomas said.

Aiden was by her side, examining her for physical damage. She turned toward him, keeping her back from view. He didn't need to know about the scratches.

"What else happened?" Dimitri spoke when Aiden stepped away from Lana.

"Lana was able to pull the demon out of Josephine and I killed it, but more will come to the city until Clover Bay is encased in an eternal darkness," he said, avoiding the subject of Donovan.

"Lana what are you keeping from us?" Benedict asked, walking around the table and placing a cold hand on the tears in her shirt. She jerked away from him, scooting closer to Professor Thomas.

He put an arm around her in protection, gaining a glare from Aiden and a halting hand from Dimitri.

"I told you tonight isn't the best night to hound her," Professor Thomas said.

Dimitri bowed his head in agreement. "Come, Benedict, Aiden, we must discuss how we are to fortify the Academy in the event that the Darkness figures out where we're hiding."

"I'll send Clara in to escort you to a room Professor Thomas. As for you Lana, you have some explaining to do in the morning," Benedict said, a sly grin forming at the corners of his mouth.

Aiden left the room first, followed by Dimitri. The three men left Lana alone with a man she'd rather not spend another moment with, although he did protect her from their wrath. In the morning, she'd have to explain why she left the Academy after having been warned multiple times of the consequences, as well as how she got the scratches on her back and what else happened in the Bay she was hiding.

She was not prepared to explain meeting Donovan, or having to face Aiden to learn his craft, but knew if she didn't, there would be no surviving what the Darkness had in store for them. Clara escorted her to her room in silence, followed by Professor Thomas who said good night to Lana before following the beautiful blonde.

That night her sleep was full of nightmares, threatening to send her over the edge and consume her with thoughts of death.

Chapter 25

Lana pulled herself out of bed, running hot water over her. The steam filled the small bathroom, making the air difficult to breathe. A knock on the door cut her shower short, Lana dressing quickly to answer.

Dimitri stood on the other side of the thick door, hands stuck in the pockets of his blue jeans.

"How did you sleep?" he asked.

"I'm not in the mood for a lecture, why are you here?" Lana said.

"We need to continue your training," Dimitri said. "Aiden is waiting in the study for us."

"Why didn't you tell me he was the other Fury?" Lana asked.

"He wasn't around when we found you, and he would not appreciate me telling his story, or any of us telling it for that matter," Dimitri said.

"I guess we shouldn't keep him waiting then," Lana said. She grabbed a jacket and followed Dimitri to the study.

"I must warn you, however, he is not very happy about this situation and will probably be very timid toward you now," Dimitri said. "I want you to forget everything you think you know about him, Lana. I know you two haven't spent much time together, but whatever you think you feel toward him will interfere with your training, and he must do the same. You will see a completely different side of him, as you did last night with Professor Thomas, but you cannot let your emotions get in the way of your training if you are to control his element. If you do, it could be very dangerous, not only for you but for him as well. Do you understand?"

He turned to her before opening the study doors. When Lana nodded, the doors opened, Aiden leaning against the wall looking out the window.

"Aiden, do you need any of us to stick around during your session?" Dimitri asked.

"I think I can handle this on my own, thanks," Aiden answered. His arms were crossed and his eyes void of emotion. "Unless you don't trust me."

"I never said I didn't trust you, I just know how you can get and I don't want there to be an accident, especially under Benedict's roof," Dimitri said. "Lana, if you need anything, just call."

He left Lana with the temperamental Fury, closing the doors behind him. The silence between them began suffocating her, leaving questions running wild through her head.

"I'm glad you brought a jacket, we won't be training in this room," Aiden said, pushing away from the window.

"We need to talk," Lana said, taking a seat at the large desk in the center of the room.

"No, actually, we don't," Aiden said, walking past her. "Until you have learned what I'm going to teach you, there will be no talking."

"So that's it then, you're just going to ignore everything that's happened?" Lana asked. Aiden whirled around, turning icy eyes on her.

"I've already been lectured by Dimitri, I don't need to be harassed by you too," Aiden said. The tension in his eyes subsided when he saw the surprise in hers. "I let my emotions get the better of me, and romanticized about a normal life and we can't let those thoughts distract us from our mission. I suggest you focus on your powers, and I will do the same."

She followed him out to a clearing in the middle of the forest. The area had target dummies placed in the form of a circle, some holding large wooden swords, others just leaned awkwardly. He sat down on the ground, crossing his legs in front of him. Placing his hands palm down on his knees, he looked up at her.

"First, you must clear your mind of any thoughts that could interfere with today's lesson," Aiden said. Lana followed suit, crossing her legs and placing her hands on her knees like she was his reflection. "Close your eyes and breathe in through your nose and out. Don't focus on your powers, just any thoughts that are distracting, or could potentially affect your emotions."

Lana did as he said, closing her eyes. When she inhaled, thoughts of Elijah and Micah in the room she'd woken up in after falling ill surfaced. She exhaled, pushing them out of her mind along with the breath from her lungs. She repeated the action, the gypsy camp coming into focus. Every time she inhaled, a new image of her previous reverie sharpened in her mind, and then rushed away as if her mind was a dam, and the floodgates had been raised, releasing every memory she'd experienced over the last twenty-four hours.

She felt water drops pelt her skin and heard them on the leaves and dirt beneath her body, as if the tears she wished would flow from her eyes were released by the clouds above.

"Clear your mind of all distracting thoughts, Lana," Aiden sighed.

Without speaking Lana returned to her breathing, focusing on the only memory she failed to remove from her mind. She saw Donovan's chest, felt his breath on her forehead. He smelled of flowers as if he'd rolled in the garden behind her home to cover up the scent of rot. His threat rang through her head.

I'd think twice before speaking to me in that tone, it may do more harm than good. Lana opened her eyes, Aiden staring back at her.

"What's keeping you from doing what I say?" Aiden asked. "This isn't a game, Lana."

"I can't do this right now, I'm sorry," Lana said, pushing herself to a standing position and walking away from the Fury.

"This isn't easy for me either, but I'm still here. I'm still trying to do what was asked of me," Aiden said, grabbing her wrist.

She turned around, pushing him away. He took hold of her wrists, keeping her close to him. "I can't be what they want me to be, and clearly I can't be what you want me to be either."

"You don't know how difficult it is for me to be here, for me to teach you how to use my power, when I can barely control it to begin with," Aiden said. "I haven't had to use my powers for centuries. I buried them away and refused to be what I am because of what I've had to do to survive. The last thing I ever wanted was to be the one to teach the next Light, and now that that person is you, all my will and control is going into keeping my anger at bay."

"Right now, I have more pressing issues to deal with than learning your craft, Aiden. The woman who practically raised me after I left the Bay is in trouble, and I left her there alone after she'd already been attacked once," Lana tried to give Aiden a reason to let her go, ensuring her troubling encounter with Donovan never came up in conversation. "Let me go back to the Bay. If I don't, the demons that attacked her will come back, if they haven't already, and this time she might not be so lucky."

"Someone else will have to take care of her because you're not leaving this place, not until it's time," Aiden said, releasing her wrists. Her hand pricked his skin, the stinging sensation lasting long enough to distract him while she ran away. It took self-control to hold him back from chasing her down. As much as he wanted to defy Dimitri, he knew there would come a time when he could feel again. He knew one day he'd make her his, he just had to destroy the Dark before she destroyed herself.

Behind closed doors she fumbled through a duffle bag in search of her phone. Once she found it, she dialed Josephine's number, hoping she'd pick up. The familiar sound of her voice on the other line made her heart slow.

"I'm glad you're alright," Lana said after Josephine swore up and down she made it home safely and could protect herself in case there would be any intruders.

"How did you know how to get that demon out of me?" Josephine asked.

"It happened to me once," Lana said, remembering the time she'd seen Aiden and another woman dancing under a cherry blossom tree right before the woman turned on him. "I remembered someone placing their hand on my chest like they were willing something to come out. There was the image of a woman in tattered clothing but she was transparent and blue. Anyway, I thought I would try it, because whatever Kyle was doing wasn't working."

"Well I'm glad you are safe as well," Josephine said. "Lana, there is something you need to know."

"What is it?" Lana's curiosity peaked.

"That demon, he had something interesting to say to me," Josephine said. "I didn't get the chance to tell you before, but it was talking about that Don character. I don't want you to worry, but I have a feeling he is somehow involved with what is coming. I know it's not something you want to hear, but I really want you to be careful, especially if he shows up again. There has to be a reason he waited so long to make contact with you, and you need to be on guard."

"Thank you, Josephine," Lana said, closing her eyes. "I have to get back to training. I'll call you when I can."

Lana hung up the phone, heading back down the stairs and out into the clearing where Aiden continued to sit on the ground breathing. She returned to her place in front of him, breathing deeply in and out, replacing the thoughts of Donovan and Josephine with rushing water which exited her mind when she exhaled.

Light danced behind her eyelids, forcing Lana to open her eyes. Aiden was tossing a ball of fire from one hand to the other. The flames dwindled until nothing but pieces of straw remained.

He placed them on the ground in front of them, grabbing a thin branch and a piece of bark from a nearby tree. "Your first lesson is on how to build a fire."

Aiden took a knife, stripping the bark from the thin branch. He twiddled it around until the tip of it was smooth and rounded at the edges. He placed the straw on top of the piece of bark and set the branch above the straw.

"Now, start with the branch between your palms, and rub them together, spinning the branch. Do it quickly," Aiden said,

Lana taking the stick from him. She did as he said, seeing smoke rise from the base of it. "Bend down and blow on the straw." Lana saw a flame flicker then die out. She repeated the steps until the flames settled. "Now go gather supplies and build your own."

Lana followed his directions, gathering straw from a nearby training dummy, tearing a piece of bark from a tree and finding a branch that was half an inch thick and about two feet long. She took his knife, picking off pieces of bark from the tip of the stick. She'd cut herself, wincing at the pain before returning to her task. Putting the bark on the ground and the straw on top of it, she held the stick between her palms, rubbing them together quickly from the top of the stick to the base in a downward motion. When smoke began to rise from the bark, she bent down and blew, causing the flame to spark to life.

Four hours were spent practicing how to make a fire by hand. He didn't speak, only focused on his breathing while she continued cutting herself, starting the fire, putting it out and starting over. By the time she'd cut her hand more than twenty times, Aiden spoke.

"That's enough for the day. Meet me back here tomorrow morning at eight," Aiden said. He stood and walked away, leaving Lana alone in the woods.

Elijah was waiting for her outside her room when she made it up the stairs.

"How was your first day of training?" he asked.

"My hands are sore and I know how to make a fire from straw, bark, and branch," Lana said. "What did you learn today?"

"I learned that Aiden needs to be careful when he speaks to you, otherwise he's going to have a very angry vampire on his back," Elijah smiled.

"Trying to protect me, I see?" Lana asked.

"I couldn't protect you from Abigale, but I can make it up to you by…"

"Never mentioning that name again?" Lana said, opening the door. "So why are you gracing me with your presence?"

"I saw Kyle and wanted to check up on you," Elijah said. "Why isn't he dead?"

Lana made herself busy with her duffle bag, packing the clothes back into it and digging for the charger to her phone. "Apparently that thing only killed the demon hunter, and now he's back to being a warlock. By the way, I went back to the Bay."

"You what? How? Why? Lana, you know it's not safe," Elijah rattled off.

"I didn't have a choice. It was either get lost in the woods or go back to a place I was familiar with," Lana said, turning to face him. "I couldn't just walk out of the study when Dimitri and Aiden were arguing about me, could I? No. I went back to my house…and my brother was there."

"Donovan, right?" Elijah asked.

"I was confused and told him to leave, and then I went to the school but the art room had been trashed. Professor Baldwin attacked me because she was possessed and so Kyle and I got it out of her but apparently it told her about him and that Donovan could be or really is involved with everything that's been going on in the Bay," Lana said.

"Slow down, you ran into your brother who you haven't seen in hundreds of years yet you told him to leave?" Elijah said. "Why would you do that?"

"He broke into my house. I hadn't seen him since my mother died. What else was I supposed to do?" Lana asked.

"Listen to what he had to say! Maybe the school wouldn't have been attacked," Elijah said.

"It wasn't Donovan, it was other demons," Lana confessed.

"But it told her about him, did it not? He could have been there to warn you, you don't know because you told him to leave," Elijah said.

"He wasn't the Donovan I remember," she said, avoiding his gaze. "He threatened me."

"What did he say?"

"You'd think twice before speaking to me in that tone, it may do more harm than good."

"Have you told Dimitri? Aiden?" Elijah asked.

She shook her head, gray eyes swelling with tears. He was there, pulling her to his chest. "You can't tell them, not until we know for sure."

"I'm scared, Eli. What if he tries to hurt her to get to me?" she asked.

"I know it sounds heartless, but it might be wise to separate yourself from her," he said, pushing her away. "At least until everything is over."

"I don't know what I'd do if anything happened to her," Lana said, wiping tears from her eyes.

"Right now, you can't afford to be distracted, and they know that. They will feed on your weaknesses, and right now Josephine is one of those weaknesses they've already touched. You need to focus on your training, do you understand?"

"You'd think I'd know that by now considering how many times I've heard it in the last day or so," Lana said. "Do you think Donovan is the leader?"

She knew the answer, but remembered what he said. No one can know.

"I hope not, for your sake," Elijah said, kissing her cheeks.

The image of her mother haunted her dreams. She saw Donovan heading out of their small home with a knife in hand, the smoke entering the building. The image of her lying on the floor of her living room looking up at him when she could not focus on his face followed, except this time he was in perfect focus. She saw a black skull instead of flesh, his dark brown eyes covered in a black film. She screamed, sitting up in bed.

She rubbed at her eyes with her knuckles, wiping sweat from her forehead. The clock across from her on the wall told her it was four in the morning. Lana slid from beneath the sheets, heading into the bathroom. She washed the remnants of her nightmare from her body, dressing in warmer clothes and heading to the clearing.

Chapter 26

By the time Aiden made it to the clearing, the dummies were covered in vines or ripped from the ground and thrown against trees. The ground beneath her feet turned to mud, reaching mid-calf for both the Furies. He knew not to approach an angry Fury from behind, making his way around to face her. She was in a different world, mumbling words he could not comprehend and swinging her arms around like she was fighting an invisible enemy.

He saw a target dummy begin to shake, coming lose from the ground and hurtling toward him. He ducked in time before it shot across the clearing and into a tree opposite of where it first existed. Aiden yelled at her but she failed to hear him.

Rain began to fall from the sky, turning the once bright morning to night with dark clouds overhead.

"Lana, you need to breathe," Aiden yelled, keeping his head low. Thunder rumbled in the sky, lightning striking the ground four inches from his face. He jumped up, grabbing hold of her shoulders. "Snap out of it before you hurt somebody." He shook her, watching the periwinkle iris fade to gray.

"Breathe, in through your nose, hold it, and exhale," he said. His grip began to burn her arms when she followed his instructions. He released her, stepping away. "Continue breathing, you need to calm down before we begin."

He picked up the dummies, placing them back in the holes they'd been in before her rampage, cleaning up the area. Debris littered the clearing and he had to pick his feet up to make it through the mud.

"Have you calmed down?" Aiden asked, standing before her. When she nodded, they left the clearing, heading further into the forest until they reached dry ground. He told her to face him, put out her hand and keep it there. He held out his hand, a small flame dancing in his palm. "Take it."

"How can you trust me?" Lana asked.

"Take the flame Lana," he said again.

"No. I just ruined your training area and you trust me enough to continue training me?"

"I told you we won't be speaking until your training is complete, now take the flame, Lana, before I make you," Aiden demanded. Lana put her hand over the flame, curling her fingers around it. She drew her hand back, holding her wrist while her flesh burned and blistered. "You're not calm. Sit down, breathe, and don't stand up until you are."

He pushed her down, walking away until he'd put ten feet between them. He leaned against a tree, tossing the flame from hand to hand. Aiden hadn't spoken about the basics of his craft since he was young, learning what he was after burning his father's throne. At first, he thought he was a witch, but Dimitri's father had already informed his family that he was not a normal creature. They sat him down, explaining that he had inherited the power of the Fury, and that he had to go away with Dimitri and the other children who'd experienced strange urges to learn their craft and how to control it.

He was always the troubled one. Aiden could never sit still long enough to focus on his breathing, something each of them had to learn. EJ, who went by Erion at the time, and Wiley spent most of their time by a lake learning how to create storms and waves, breezes and puddles. Dimitri spent his time in the forest learning about soil and seed, flora and even how to speak to animals. Aiden was locked in a dungeon, the only place he could practice his skills and not harm anyone or burn anything down.

Not only did they learn how to use their powers, they also learned how to fight. Each of them was given a weapon. Aiden had a copper sword with a gold and black hilt, and spent days sharpening it before every competition in which they fought each other, testing their abilities as well as their expertise in hand to hand combat.

"Aiden?" Lana said, waking him from his reverie.

"Take the flame," he said, tossing it back and forth in his hands. She sat in front of him, concentrating on the heat. She closed her eyes, imagined the ball of fire in her hand, and reached out for it, feeling the heat in her palm, and curling her fingers around it. It didn't burn her this time and when she opened her eyes, it was slithering in and out of her fingers. When it disappeared, she heard him say do it again.

Each time she tried, he'd made it more difficult. At one point, she was chasing them through the forest, jumping up and down, weaving in and out of trees like will-o-the-wisps. When she caught the fireball, he conjured three more. Each ball had more and more power she was required to catch. When she would chase one ball, the other two would dart after her. She chased them like a dog chases a tennis ball, catching them, bringing them back to her owner and dashing after them again and again until exhaustion consumed her.

Day after day he'd send her fetching fireballs, never once telling her how to make them herself. Lana ran until her feet hurt, dodging fire like a cop dodges bullets during a shootout.

Scorched clothes, skin, and hair, scratches from sliding across the ground and bruises from when she'd slam into a tree or a rock reminded her each day of the battle she would one day have to fight when Darkness invaded her life.

"That's enough for today. Meet back here at normal time," Aiden said, walking toward the clearing.

"When am I going to learn how to make my own fire?" Lana asked.

"You already know how to make a fire," he said, hiding a smile.

"I mean, when am I going to be able to throw fire like you do or create lava or…"

"You will never learn that skill, do you understand me?" he said, whirling around to face her. She had been breathing hard, trying to catch her breath after having spent the day sprinting through the forest.

"Why not? If I'm supposed to be what everyone expects me to, I have to learn what you do," Lana said.

"You will learn what I do when I think you're ready," Aiden said, glaring down at her. "Right now, you're not strong enough, and you're sure as hell not ready to face them."

"Then make me ready. You're the only thing standing between me and the Light," Lana said, putting her hands on her hips. "Why won't you let me learn what you're supposed to be teaching me?"

"Because if I do," *I could lose you forever.* "If you see the Light, the Darkness will destroy you."

Aiden transported from the clearing and into one of the practice rooms of the Academy. His cheeks filled with heat, his heart thumping like the hind paw of Thumper in Bambi. He tried to concentrate on his breathing but instead his fingers tingled with power, sparking to life. His arms were covered in flames when he swung them toward a glass target. Instead of shattering, it turned into water, making the fire fizz out. He threw fireball after fireball at the target until the flames died out, sinking to his knees with his head in his hands. For weeks, he'd sent Lana running in circles, trying to postpone the inevitable.

He wished he could show her why he did not want her to know his skill, wanted to take her back to 1452, the day the Diviner Leressi betrayed him and the others, bringing the Darkness into their kingdom. But Aiden knew that with great power, comes great responsibility, responsibility and power she did not understand nor want to begin with. He saw the way she ran from his power, rather than confront it and embrace it, even though that is what he told her to do.

Aiden knew if she saw the Light and reached for it, there was a chance she would not only kill the leader of the Darkness, but she would also kill herself. He and the others had never known what came of Arin after her light lit the sky. The Furies rushed through a portal created by the Headmaster, leaving Sumardana and their people behind. Someone had to survive, he told himself. Someone had to find the next Amethyst before the Darkness, and Dimitri had done just that. As much as Aiden hated him for keeping her a secret, he knew it was worth keeping it a secret.

He met Dimitri and Wiley in the study, updating them on how Lana's training was going.

"Where is EJ?" Aiden asked.

The other Furies were quiet. He'd focused on her training and forgotten about his friend's dwindling health.

"Can't the Elder help him?" Aiden asked, raising his voice.

"EJ has passed, Aiden," Dimitri said softly, looking up into the Fire Fury's face. "We will be holding a funeral tomorrow."

"Why didn't you tell me?"

"You needed to focus, and we knew telling you would ruin your focus," Wiley said. "EJ would have wanted you to complete her training so we can destroy the Darkness once and for all."

"And what if they attack?"

"We expected them to attack within days of our arrival yet they have refrained from doing so. I think we're safe for one more day," Wiley said.

"Benedict has done well in keeping the wards secure, keeping everyone within the Academy grounds safe," Dimitri said. "I imagine we should not push our luck any further and should expect an attack within the next few days. If anything, we need to monitor all creatures entering and leaving the premises."

"And if they don't attack?" Aiden asked.

"What is next on the agenda with Lana's training?" Dimitri asked.

Chapter 27

Lana sat on the bench of the gazebo, staring out at the pastures. Donovan approached, taking a seat across from her.

"I knew you'd find me again," Lana said.

"Why aren't you somewhere safe?"

"I had to see you again," Lana turned to face him. "I still have so many questions to ask you."

"There's no time for questions, Lana." Donovan leaned forward. "They're planning an attack, and I don't know when. They've been keeping things from me ever since you left town."

"Who is 'they'?" Lana asked.

"The Elders, the ones who trained me and helped me build the Dark Army. Lana, they're planning something big and I don't know if you or your team can handle it."

"We've run out of time," Lana said.

"From what I've been told, you've also lost one of your teammates," Donovan said.

"What are you talking about?"

"Matthew attacked one of the Furies when you all left town, and he was badly injured. There is a rumor swirling in the Underworld that he has passed away."

"What? He can't!"

"That's how we die, Lana. We kill each other... It had to happen, that is life."

"But, I still have so much to learn!"

"Lana, calm down."

"No, I can't calm down. He was my friend. Don..."

"Lana, I need you to return to your safe house, do you understand?"

"Will you stop asking me if I understand? I don't! I never will!"

"Go, now. The others will be waiting for you. They need you."

Lana didn't wait for another order, she returned to the Academy right before Dimitri knocked on her bedroom door.

"May I come in?" he asked. Lana nodded.

They took a seat on the edge of her bed, Dimitri inhaling deeply before speaking.

"Tomorrow, there will be a..." Dimitri choked. "The day you left the club house, a member of the Darkness attacked EJ. He was badly injured, and as we expected he has passed away."

Lana didn't want what Donovan had told her to be true. "But I was harmed by the Darkness and I survived... How could he not?"

"The Elder did all he could to prevent death, but EJ was not strong enough."

Dimitri stood, placing his hand on the wall to brace himself. "There will be a funeral tomorrow morning in the cemetery across from the training clearing. I understand if you prefer to focus on your training, but Era would appreciate it if you attended. We all would."

Lana nodded, Dimitri exiting the room. There was no telling what would happen at the funeral, if this is when the

Darkness planned on attacking. She didn't know, but what she did know was that she could no longer rely on Donovan for information as his own army was keeping him in the dark on their plans of attack.

~

A white casket sat on rails meant to lower it into the ground in the center of a crowd. Closed per Era's request, the casket held the remains of a great warrior, Dimitri said in his speech.

"Erion was a good friend, a great mentor, and a tremendous warrior," the Earth Fury stated. "It is never easy saying goodbye, but such is the way of life. Such is our way of life. Erion served dutifully, selflessly, and with honor."

Era dotted her eyes with tissues, unable to hold back her tears. EJ was her lover, her confidant, someone she knew would come home every day and would protect her from the evil that hunted Diviners.

"He was a loving husband, a less than perfect son, and the best friend we all needed in times of crisis," Wiley said. "He defended Era and Lana with his life when the Darkness so rudely invaded our home."

"Wiley…" Dimitri said.

Era's sobs grew louder.

"EJ will be remembered for years to come," Aiden concluded. "To our brother, may he rest in peace."

"Help!" a small dark headed girl being pushed to the ground beneath the weight of another dark headed individual yelled. When Lana looked over, her heart sank into her chest, nauseating her. Getting out of her seat, Rae and Elijah pulled at her wrists but she resisted, walking slowly to the door.

"Aleana," she heard faintly. Her pace picked up to a jog until she was next to the boy. She rolled him over, blood smearing her hands. His face held scratches like the ones she'd obtained from the demon in Josephine, bruises stained his eyes and blood ran from his ears, eyes and nose.

Aiden and Elijah picked her up by her armpits, pulling her away kicking and screaming from Donovan.

"No, he's my brother, he needs my help," Lana yelled, pushing the men off her. She dropped to her knees, pushing on his chest to wake him. She felt his heart beat weakly beneath her palms.

Elijah pulled her back to her feet again, wrapping his arms around her waist and crunching her ribs when she fought back. "Remember what Josephine said, Lana. Remember what I said."

Clara placed a finger to his temple, extracting his last memory for review. She saw demons, vampires, and witches around him, an old gentleman with white hair and dark eyes holding a staff embellished with skulls made of bone and an onyx gemstone at its tip. A horned demon picked him up, throwing him against a wall. Lifting him off the ground, the demon released talons from his fingers, slashing his face from temple to jaw line.

"You're a disgrace," the old man said, pointing his staff at Donovan. The gemstone glowed silver and gold with dark magic. The horned demon took the ring off his hand, placing it in the palm of the Elder. "You better warn the girl. I hope you make it to her before I do."

Clara stood, turning to Lana who continued to fight the vampire holding her back. "He's been communicating with the Dark Elders, but they exiled him. He's here to warn you that they are coming. They know where we are."

Elijah dragged Lana away from the funeral and into the clearing, following Benedict.

"Well, Dimitri, what is your plan?" Benedict asked.

"We will take Lana to the club house. Aiden burned it down so they won't be looking for us to return there. Donovan will be coming with us as well," Dimitri said.

"And what if they attack while you are playing around with your tails between your legs?"

"What do you expect us to do? Stay and fight? You said it yourself, you do not want anything bad to come of this place. This is our chance to lead them away from the Academy. If we do not, all you've worked for will have been lost," Dimitri said.

"They took away my home, my family. We ran once before, but I'm not going to run this time."

"I'm not asking you to, friend. I'm asking you to protect these children while we take care of this problem," the Emerald said.

"You won't get the chance to run," Donovan said, clutching his stomach. "They've already surrounded the place."

Lana took advantage of Elijah's surprise, slipping out of his grip and facing Donovan. "Why are you here? What good are you, warning us about their attack if they've already got us cornered?"

"They told me to come here, Aleana," Donovan said, Lana grimacing at the way he said her name. "I'm no threat to you, they've taken my ring. I've never had the privilege of learning how to control my powers without it. It's the Elders you must worry about now. They know the Darkness in and out, and he's coming for your power. You of all people are in the most danger."

"The prophecy says you have to destroy the Darkness," Wiley said. "If he's the Darkness, kill him."

"You realize what you're asking me to do, right?" Lana twirled till she faced the Water Fury.

"He is not your brother, he is the enemy." Wiley's face was so close she felt his breath on her eyelashes.

"I know you have no reason to trust me. But I know their weaknesses, and I can help you if you let me. You will need it if you are to *reach* for the Light," Donovan said. Aiden's patience had worn thin. He grabbed the bloody man by his neck, pushing his head to the ground.

"Aiden stop, he has a point," Dimitri spoke. "If he speaks the truth, if he has no way to access his power, we have an advantage we will desperately need if we are to stand a chance against these Elders. Considering you haven't taught Lana a single thing, she has no way of even seeing the Light."

"I can't teach someone something when that someone doesn't want anything to do with this life," Aiden said, releasing Donovan.

"It's not that I don't want to, it's that you have some ill-conceived notion that something bad will happen to me if I do," Lana said, turning on him. "You have no idea what will happen to me if I produce that big bright light in the sky. You weren't there!"

"It doesn't matter if I was with Arin or not, the point is you don't stand a chance, no Amethyst has ever stood a chance against the Darkness and you will be no exception to the rule," Aiden said, his face was inches from her, his eyes dancing with fire. Lana concentrated on what Dimitri said once when he was teaching her how to conjure the elements of the earth.

She closed her eyes, breathing in and out like Aiden had told her the first day of her training with him, imagined the ball of fire he tossed from hand to hand while she calmed down. She had grabbed the heat, feeling it dance in and out of her fingers. She felt the heat coming to her hands, opening her eyes. A light orange ring played with her iris.

"I told you, you already know how to make a fire," Aiden said softly. He drew a circle in the air, telling her to turn around. Each of the training dummies burst into flames, the shadows dancing. The heat retreated the longer she stared at her manifestation.

"You didn't tell me I could do this," Lana sighed.

Bells rang three times, signifying that intruders had made their way into the infirmary.

Dimitri left the clearing, Wiley following. Aiden took Lana by the arm, nodding toward Donovan. The three of them followed suit, meeting the other Furies in the study. Benedict waved his hand, placing Elijah, Micah, Rae, and Christine among them in the large library.

"We need to keep those demons from the hall. If we don't at least try to protect them, Benedict will never forgive me for bringing us into his home," Dimitri said.

"Micah and I can take Donovan to the infirmary. That should distract them long enough for you guys to get outside and lead them away from the Academy," Elijah said.

"I didn't sign up for this, brother. I'm not putting my life on the line for them," Micah nodded in the direction of the dining room.

"What about for me?" Lana said, crossing her arms across her chest. Micah stared at her for a moment, surprised at her remark.

"That's not fair," he said. "You know I would."

"Well then maybe you should get going. If you don't, I could lose my life, and then what would you do?" Lana tilted her head to the left, smiling and then turning toward Aiden and the others. Elijah and Micah left the study, heading toward the infirmary with their Dark guest.

"We'll head to the barn," Dimitri said, the boys nodding in agreement.

"What about us?" Rae asked.

"You're going back to the hall," Dimitri said. He flicked his hand, the girls disappearing in a green haze that returned them to the hall. Aiden and Lana exchanged glances before he took her hand, the four of them leaving the Academy in search of the barn.

They landed on the floor of the forest surrounded by thick bushes, cursing under their breath. They'd made it out of the Academy but remained far from their destination, continuing on foot. The moon was blacked out by dark clouds, summoning demons from the underworld. Lana chased after the other Furies who now had weapons in their hands.

Aiden's copper sword, Dimitri's oak staff covered in vines, and Wiley's trident ripped through sheaths that let out deafening shrieks. Lana's staff formed in her hands, the amethyst tip pulsing with power. She'd never seen it pulse before, wondering if it was now because of her new ability to conjure fire.

Horned demons with snake tongues, vampires with gray skin instead of white and witches blocked their path to the barn. They had formed a protective barrier around the grounds of the Academy, forcing the Furies to fight. The three elementals formed a protective semi-circle around Lana, breaking bones and slicing off heads when any Dark creature came near them. They pushed their way toward the barn, breaking through the barrier.

"That was too easy," Wiley said, spinning his trident around. He looked toward the Academy, its steeples still intact.

The ground began to rumble, creating thick gashes in the earth.

Lana, if you remember anything from your training, it should be to stay balanced. Think of what you've seen us do, and try to replicate it. Aiden's power will be your strongest, yet weakest advantage if you can remember to breathe, Lana heard in her head. The ground rose beneath them, driving them into the air before disappearing, sending them plummeting toward the hard earth.

Chapter 28

Lana searched the field for signs of the other Furies, her head pounding after landing hard on the floor of the forest. She found nothing but disturbed soil and demons. Muffled by bark and leaves, the sounds of sword on sword drifted on the wind to her. She knew who was still fighting.

A red and yellow demon with tusks and horns protruding from its neck formed a club with spikes in its hand, heading toward her. She hopped to her feet, inhaling deeply before pulling a chunk of dirt from the field, hurling it in his direction. It hit the demon in the leg, tripping him. Another creature charged at her from her right, its weapon greeting hers when she lifted it in front of her to block the attack.

It had scraggly hair, a face full of rotting skin and empty pits for eyes. She wondered how it found her with no vision. The arch of her foot met the creature's spine, shattering it into pieces. Lana swung the staff above her head, hitting its skull like a baseball. It dissipated into black dust, the soil beneath where it scattered rotting away.

The tusk and horn demon was on its feet heading toward her. She felt branches and leaves tickle her skin, vines wrapping around her arms. Like spider webs, she released them, each tendril taking a limb from the demon and pulling them in opposite directions until the demon tore in four pieces.

With each creature vanquished more dust fell upon the field, and rot took over until she was standing in a graveyard.

The Furies joined her in the field, heaving from exertion. Blood stained their clothes, weapons from the recent events.

"Bravo, bravo," a figure in a black cloak clapped. "Tell me, Aleana, where did you learn to fight like that?"

The figure released his hood, revealing wrinkled skin, tired and old eyes and a white head of hair. When the man smiled, his teeth were black and rotted away. "Donovan has told me so much about you, my dear. It's a shame he couldn't be here to see you all grown up."

"Why waste our time talking?" Lana said, twirling her staff in her hand. She pointed the tip toward the ground, its gemstone pulsing a bright lavender color. The man flicked his hands, sending a swirl of darkness toward them. Lana placed her staff to her chest to block the smoke which burned like acid, just like Josephine had burned Kyle.

She closed her eyes, focusing on the breeze she'd felt when they ran through the forest. She imagined she was back in her living room when the smoke choked her. Without opening her eyes, she felt a strong wind diffuse the acid in the fog, creating a black tornado from the man's attack. She sent it in his direction, hearing a gasp and imagining him rolling out of its way.

He charged her, a black skull-encrusted staff forming in his hand. An onyx stone created a sharp arrowhead at its tip. She smelled a strong aroma of decaying garbage as he neared, taking a few steps back to prepare for the blow. When she put her staff up to block the initial attack, it shattered in two, sending her backward, sliding over the rotting soil.

Aiden's arms erupted in flames, Lana watching him intently. He placed his palms together, pulled them apart and around in a circle, creating and pushing the fireball between them in the direction of the Elder. It knocked him off his feet, sizzling his skin and catching his robes on fire. Aiden's sword was in his hand once more, the blade surrounded by a ring of fire.

The Elder was on his feet quickly, countering Aiden's every attack. The two fighters swayed and swung, dodged, blocked and rolled out of the way before Lana grabbed the two pieces of her staff. She spun them around in her hands, reinforcing the wood with vines and fire, like Aiden's blade.

Aiden dodged a swing but not before the Elder had the chance to conjure another black smoke, forcing it to shroud the Ruby Fury. She saw him stagger backward, dropping his sword. It disappeared, leaving only charred ground beneath. Lana grasped one piece of her staff like a javelin, sending it flying toward the Elder, piercing his right shoulder.

Next Wiley jumped into the fight, creating a torrential downpour above the Elder. Lana forced her hand to the sky, Lightning striking down all around them. Dimitri was nowhere to be found, leaving Lana to fend against vampires and witches while the other Furies kept their enemy busy. She returned her attention to them, pulling a chunk of soil from the ground, hopping onto it to attain a higher vantage point. The witches, stuck to the ground, fired spell after spell in her direction, from fire bolts to dark fog and lightning bolts, each one being deflected.

Lana followed EJ's direction, feeling the surge of electricity in her fingertips. She pointed her palm in the direction of the witches, releasing bolts of electricity from her palms. They erupted in white dust, leaving the vampires as her only other enemy. They sprinted at her, leaping from the ground. She front-flipped off the platform, landing on the ground. She let her knees buckle, rolling on the ground into a standing position, the vampires behind her. They were flown into a tree before they realized she'd jumped off.

They darted toward her, meeting Elijah and Micah in their way. The vampires, blurs of black and white, threw each other into trees, disappearing into the forest.

Aleana, you need to get out of here, Lana heard in her head. Donovan was near, making Lana search the tree line for sign of him. She felt heat at her fingertips, feeling the flames engross them, and wrapping around her wrists and up her forearms. She turned in the direction of the Elder who was on his knees, his lips moving uncontrollably.

He pulled his arms into his chest and then jerked them apart abruptly, sending Wiley into the barn wall to his left. He fixed his black, heartless eyes onto Lana. She pulled her arms back as if getting ready to throw a baseball, followed through with the throw and let two melon-sized fireballs free in the Elder's direction.

They threw him off guard but he charged her regardless. She continued to throw ball after ball, chunk of dirt after chunk of dirt until he was close enough to touch. Kneeling, she grabbed a fistful of dirt, standing and raising her hands above her head. A barrier of mud and rock formed above her, forcing the Elder to fight his way through. She closed her eyes, reaching for the dark clouds above. They dissipated from a black veil into dark gray cotton candy puffs, rumbling low with thunder and lighting the field with bursts of Lightning. She curled her fingers into fists, pulling them down slowly. The clouds let out a lout crack, raining down Lightning and fire all around her barrier.

Dimitri and Donovan watched the scene unfold while they helped the other Furies out of their graves and into the barn.

The Elder, tiring and growing angry, stuck both hands through the rock wall, sending a plague through it that cracked and shattered it. Lana's eyes locked onto his, the irises a pinwheel of color and surprise.

He grabbed her by the neck with one hand, thrusting the other hand through her stomach. She could feel her bones breaking when he grabbed hold of her spine. Dimitri and the others had to hold Aiden down as he started to seize, feeling everything being done to Lana, while they watched their Amethyst fade before them.

"You, much like your brother, are a disgrace to your kind," the Elder hissed.

Aleana, let the blackness wash over you. Close your eyes, she heard.

I see mother, Don.

Look past her, are you in the tunnel?

Yes, I can be with her again.

I need you to reach into the tunnel, Aleana. Reach into the tunnel until you see the light.

Lana did as he said, reaching past the Elder. She saw a bright light, the silhouette of her mother being over powered by it.

Don't let go of it until you can feel it in your hand.

A small pearl of light touched her palm, forcing Lana to pull it into her. She let it seep into her body, searching for more directions. When Donovan hadn't answered her plea, she let her instincts fall over her. She opened her eyes, a gold iris staring into a black skull with no eyes and skin melting off the bone. She placed her hands on his body, pushing the power out of her.

Every bone in her body felt like it was shattering into a million pieces, turning her into gold fragments like when she destroyed a demon. She felt her skin prickle with energy, making the hair stand up and sending shockwaves down her spine.

Another loud noise rang through the forest, like a bomb had been set off. The Furies watched as Lana became a beacon of light, sending a wave of energy through the forest. Every demon, witch, and creature affiliated with the Darkness exploded, leaving no trace of their existence except a piece of jewelry that bounced off the rocks around the fire pit.

Chapter 29

Her eyes fluttered beneath her eyelids, remembering the battle. She could feel the warmth within her, could see the light in front of her. She knew the only way to end the pain was to reach for it. The light swirled into a small sphere, hurling itself toward her open palm. When she felt the pearl of power she wrapped her fingers around it, drawing it within her.

Lana pushed the power from the inside out, setting off an atomic bomb in the field. Within seconds, the Dark apprentices disintegrated until only clouds of dust remained in their place, taking her brother with them. There was no amount of remediation or redemption that could save him from the Light. She saw his face then, saw the skin melt off the bone and reveal black spheres for eyes. His jaw opened wide and let out a scream that deafened her, shaking her awake.

When she opened her eyes, she stared at tattered tapestries hanging over the remains of a decrepit wooden canopy bed frame. She lay still in the unfamiliar room. There was a window that had been boarded up to the east, letting small strands of light in from outside. Layers of dust covered torn curtains attached to a splintering rod leaning against the cracked concrete wall.

To the west next to the bed sat a small circular table with a candle lighting the small room, the smell of dirt and moist wood in the air. In the doorway another tattered curtain, burn marks on the edges trailing the ground, separated the room from the outside world. She heard the material rustle, turning her head to see who entered the room.

"You're awake," Aiden said softly, walking to sit next to her on the bed. She moved slowly, her body aching from the events of her nightmare. He took her hand, hoping she wouldn't pull away and rubbed his thumb against her soft skin. "I was worried about you."

"I'm sorry," Lana said softly.

"You did nothing wrong," he said, raising his eyes to meet hers. "I wanted so desperately for you to be human that I refused to train you and put your wellbeing at risk. But I am relieved you're not human."

"Why are you relieved?" she asked.

"Because humans don't understand us, and I'm not like the others. I can't…trust the Diviners, although they have done wonders to Dimitri and the others regarding their tempers," he rambled. "The prophecy has always been that Light will destroy Dark, but it's always been implied that Light is destroyed in the process yet here you are, here we are…" Aiden paused. "I don't know what I would do if you were not here."

His eyes were a light turquoise, but looked dark blue in the low lighting.

"I haven't felt the way I feel about you in a very long time, and it terrifies me," Lana said, a tear slipping down her cheek.

Aiden reached to wipe the tear away. He caught her chin as Lana turned her head away, carefully turning it back toward him. "Please don't be afraid of me."

He cupped her cheek in his hand, wiping the tears away that continued to fall. Leaning in, she closed her eyes as their lips touched. His were softer than she imagined, comforting her as she leaned into him. She pictured their first kiss in a different setting with him walking her to her door after taking her on a date. He would lean in to give her a good night kiss on the cheek as she stood perched against the doorframe, him pushing his weight against the wall behind her. Instead, he would kiss her lips, but somehow this felt more natural.

Lana felt heat on her lips, pulling away slightly. She opened her eyes to see Aiden watching her carefully. She touched her lips when the warmth faded; confused at the odd sensation she felt when she kissed him.

"So, you felt that too," he smiled. "You don't know how long I've wanted to do that."

"I imagined us somewhere different," Lana smiled. She could feel herself blushing, grateful the candle only lit the corner. "Speaking of which, where are we exactly?"

Aiden dropped his head, squeezing her hand.

He helped her out of bed, letting her lean against him. The pressure of her against his side was light when she wrapped her arm around his back, gripping at his right side. His hand slid down to the small of her back when they walked back through the burnt curtain. Her breath caught in her throat when she looked around, seeing broken trade carts with ripped and burned covers all around, foliage grew from the ground, attached itself to the crumbled walls and on top of the roofs.

Lana saw a fire rumbling before her, feeling the chill of the wind in the forest. Adobe huts dotted the landscape, all crumbling to pieces. The huts that were still in livable shape had been occupied by the Diviners she figured when she saw Wiley and Dimitri tossing around a ball of some sort. The roofs were once made of branches, cloth, and straw for insulation but were burned to ashes. The trees which surrounded the small town were not as tall as the trees behind them, telling her that this part of the forest had once been burned to the ground, but years of abandonment allowed them to grow back bigger, brighter, and fuller than before.

"What is this place?" Lana asked, looking up at Aiden who had been watching her reactions.

"Welcome to Sumardana," Aiden said quietly.